TH
BOSCOMBE
BOYS

Mark Fuidge

"If there's a book that you want to read, but it hasn't been written yet, then you must write it."
— **Toni Morrison**

Chapter One

From my hiding place in the bushes, I stared through the leaves at the black leather biker boots that had appeared on the woodland path in front of me. I'd hoped to see a pair of white, size eleven stilettos, belonging to my new roommate Bull, but instead, my eyes focused on the buckle straps that ran up the front of the gnarly footwear as I tried to recall seeing anyone at the '80s themed house party dressed as The Terminator.

With dawn fast approaching I'd decided to take the shortcut through the woods. A metallic screech, I'd heard moments earlier, alerted me to the presence of someone and I'd stopped to hide, hoping Bull would soon catch me up in his Tina Turner outfit.

I was reminded of the games of hide and seek I used to play with my grandad when I was little. He would get on his hands and knees and crawl around the house looking for me. I'd always hide in the same place — the wardrobe in the bedroom. I'd wait excitedly in black silence.

Then the dull thuds would begin as he came up the wooden stairs, slapping each one for dramatic effect. It worked. My heart would race faster as he inched his way across the landing — then silence. I'd wait in the darkness, taking slow, shallow breaths, desperate for the game to end as the bedroom door slowly creaked open. The thudding would resume louder than ever. I knew it was only my grandad, but in my mind, I imagined a terrifying monster getting ready to pounce. The thuds became deafening, and before he could find me, I'd burst out of the wardrobe and leap into his arms. The game was over and I couldn't have been happier.

Desperate for this game to end, I prepared to jump out of my hiding place when I noticed something glisten next to the boots. It was the blade of a shiny new spade. Adrenaline shot through my veins.

I heard a Zippo lighter ping open — tobacco smoke began to overpower the crisp woodland air. I remained motionless. One snapped twig now and I'd have to explain what I was doing hiding in the woods at five o'clock in the morning dressed as Rambo.

If only I'd waited for Bull to finish off the last of the scrumpy. It had been a surreal sight, seeing him in a blonde wig, ill-fitting leopard print dress and stilettos, holding the plastic barrel above his head trying to finish off the last dregs. But I needed at least a few hours sleep before The Freshers Ball the following night and decided to head back to our student house in Boscombe.

I'd moved in a few days earlier with all my worldly possessions — a bin liner full of clothes, a duvet, a packet of cheap Turkish cigarettes and a book on palm reading which I hoped would help me woo a few of the more adventurous female freshers.

The book had come with a free gold-plated necklace and small pendant in the shape of a palmistry hand which now dangled around my neck. It twinkled in my peripheral vision and I quietly clasped it in my fist.

The lighter snapped shut and through a gap in the leaves, I saw a man's blood-soaked hand place it into the pocket of a dark green trench coat before he continued on his journey. My eyes followed and as he came into full view further down the path my relief turned to horror. Slung over his shoulder was a large object, wrapped in a dark grey tarpaulin. I watched, terrified, as he disappeared deeper into the woods.

*

"Fudge...Fudge...Fudgey...Wake up!!"

Keeping my eyes shut, I desperately tried to remain asleep.

"Come on, Fudge, it's eleven o'clock, fancy going for a fry up? We need some fuel in the tank if we're gunna make it through today," Bull said in his broad Birmingham accent.

Images from the previous night flashed through my mind — flaming sambucas, shell suits, tequila slammers, blonde wigs, lager, tequila worm, barrel of scrumpy, shiny spade, blood-soaked hand. My eyes sprang open only to be confronted by Bull's thick, hairy legs thrusting out of the skin-tight, leopard print dress he was still wearing. He stood over me and picked up a book from my bedside table.

"What the fok is this? *The Beginner's Guide to Palm Reading.* You don't believe in any of this rubbish, do you?" he said returning it to the table.

"Oh no, I thought it would be a good way to chat up the ladies or at least give me an excuse to hold their hands," I replied, slightly embarrassed, before quickly changing the subject.

"Mate, I think I saw something terrible in the woods on the way back from the party."

"Not doggers?"

"No, there was a man. His hand was covered in blood. He had a spade and was carrying something wrapped in tarpaulin over his shoulder."

I paused before dramatically adding, "I think it was a dead body."

"Shut up!! You must have dreamt it. I walked through the woods not long after you. I'm sure I'd have noticed someone carrying a dead body."

"I wish I had dreamt it."

Bull walked back to his bed, retrieved the contact lenses he'd placed overnight in a glass of water on his bedside table and began placing them back in his eyes.

"You did eat the worm from that tequila bottle. They say that's a hallucinogenic."

I vaguely recalled the incident.

"It might have been the worm, but it felt real enough. Do you think I should call the police?"

"And say what? You got paralytic last night, ate a hallucinogenic worm and saw someone in the woods carrying a dead body?"

I thought for a moment.

"I suppose you're right."

"Come on then, do you fancy going for a nice fry-up?"

"Yeah, are you getting changed?"

"No, mate, it's The Freshers Ball tonight, it will save us coming back later."

Still wearing my combat outfit, I got out of bed, picked up my black wig off the floor, repositioned it on my head and went to the bathroom to splash some cold water on my face. Looking up from the sink into the mirror, I hardly recognised myself as I swished back the long synthetic hair with a shake of my head.

Out on the landing, Bull knocked on the other two bedroom doors to see if our new housemates wanted to join us.

"Jim, Micky," he shouted.

When neither yielded a response, we stumbled downstairs and headed out through the kitchen at the back of the house. We'd only moved in a few days ago and already a mountain of dirty crockery sat in the sink, and the bin was overflowing with various takeaway containers. We stopped at a traffic light near the back door which had just changed from green to red.

"What on earth is that doing in here?" I asked.

"Fok knows. It's one of those temporary traffic lights you get at road works," replied Bull. "How can it still be working?"

We followed a yellow cable that trailed out through the back door, down the driveway and out onto the road where we found some minor road works, another traffic light and a large industrial battery pack. Thankful no traffic was on the quiet back road, we quickly returned it to where it belonged.

"Who do you think did that?" asked Bull as we headed off towards the high street.

"Well, to be fair, the state we were all in last night it could have been any one of us."

We struggled to recall our final movements of the previous night. Jim and Micky were prime suspects, but before we could come to any conclusion a sign in an off-licence window distracted us.

"Five-gallon barrel of scrumpy only twenty pounds," shouted Bull excitedly.

"Yeah, I bet it tastes like battery acid."

"Perfect, that's just the way I like it."

Pressing our faces against the window we stared at the barrels of scrumpy stacked up inside. A large lady stepped out of a nearby doorway followed by a warm pungent smell of stale cooking oil. The sign above her head read The Halloween Café. We shuffled along and began peering through its window. Toy spiders, plastic skulls and witches on broomsticks dangled from the ceiling. Several eerie paintings hung on the walls. It wasn't clear if the cobwebs in the corners were real or fake. Without a word, we looked at each other and nodded.

Inside, a rotund man in soiled chef's whites stood behind a well-used serving counter swigging a can of strong European lager. Behind him was an open plan kitchen where a line of cooking appliances along the right-hand wall bellowed out a wave of heat that oozed over the counter into the eating area. On the left-hand side was a selection of fridges and freezers, all covered in a fine layer of yellow grease, desperately trying to shield their contents from the heatwave.

Flames flickered out from two large eye-level grills. A blackened frying pan sat on a large gas ring occasionally spitting out hot oil as it waited to frazzle its next victim. Underneath this were the metal doors of a double oven. To one side was a deep fat fryer, its wire basket sat just above the boiling oil waiting to plunge in its next payload. Either side of a closed-door at the back of the kitchen hung some eerily realistic skeletons of varying sizes.

"Blimey, what have we got 'ere then? Rambo and his missus?" he bellowed as he stealthily hid his drink behind the counter.

I gave a half-hearted explanation for our appearance whilst scanning a laminated menu. The dishes were aptly named — Spook-getti Bolognaise, Hungarian Ghoul-ash. We opted for two Frightening Fry-ups, grabbed a couple of newspapers from the rack on the wall and sat down by the window.

A burly man with thinning ginger hair entered the café sporting large mirrored sunglasses, a rugged camouflage jacket and a pair of old black work trousers which were pulled over the top of a pair of muddy boots.

He ordered beans on toast and made his way over to the table in the far corner. My eyes were drawn to his boots. Poking out from the bottom of his trousers was a familiar-looking buckle strap.

Instinctively I looked up. Unsure if he was staring at me, I noticed my panicked reflection in his sunglasses. A bedraggled waitress appeared and slid two plates of fry-ups onto the table.

I turned to Bull and whispered.

"That bloke in the corner was staring at me."

"Well, it's not often Rambo and his wife come in here for breakfast," Bull replied without even looking up from his newspaper.

Behind me, I heard someone else enter the café. A stocky man in a scruffy denim jacket brushed past me. His large bald head shimmered with a thin layer of sweat and I couldn't help but gawp at the tattoo of a pair of angel's wings that covered the back of his scalp. He made his way towards the man in the corner and sat down opposite him as I continued to marvel at the impressive ink work.

Slowly, I unravelled my cutlery from a cheap paper napkin whilst secretly listening to the conversation that had begun.

"Did you manage to bury her?" whispered the newcomer.

My knife and fork clattered noisily onto the table as the words swirled around my head. The conversation stopped and I could feel them both staring at me as I fumbled to pick up my cutlery. Without looking up I started to eat. Their voices lowered, but I could still hear them.

"The ground was quite soft so it didn't take long to dig the hole."

The room began to spin. I clumsily placed my knife and fork down and gripped the sides of the table.

"No one saw you then?"

"No, thank goodness, the last thing I wanted was coppers everywhere."

Bull's knife glistened as it cut into his sausage. I looked again at the boots. Whilst I studied them the waitress appeared and gave him a plate of beans on toast.

"Here you go, love."

"Cheers," he said pushing his sleeves up.

Angry red scratches covered his exposed forearms, and I instantly felt beads of sweat accumulate on my forehead.

"Lost your appetite?" asked Bull.

"It wasn't a dream," I managed to blurt out.

"Eh? What are you going on about? Are you going to eat that?"

I pushed my plate towards Bull as the man wearing the sunglasses reached inside his jacket. Still, the conversation remained barely above a whisper.

"Thanks for letting me borrow your motor," he said handing over a set of keys.

Consumed with a myriad of emotions I watched as the bald man took the keys then handed over a folded piece of paper.

Without a word, it was unfolded and carefully examined. From the reflection in the sunglasses, I caught a glimpse of a man's face on the paper before it was folded back up and put into the pocket of his jacket. I felt like I was in a movie, but hadn't been given the script.

The bald man leant forward.

"Find him, do the business and there'll be a nice little payout for you."

In a daze, I managed to say, "fresh air."

Getting to my feet I walked unsteadily outside and sat down on a nearby bench. Putting my head in my hands I cast my mind back to the previous night. My recollection was hazy at best, but I was convinced they were the same boots. And the fresh scratches on his arms would certainly account for the blood I saw.

*

Bull emerged from the café and sat down next to me.

"Alright, matey, are you ok?"

"That bloke in the café."

"Which one?"

"The one with the sunglasses."

"Oh yeah."

"He's a killer."

"What?"

"He's an assassin."

"What? Are you still tripping on that worm?"

9

"I'm sure he's the bloke in the woods last night. I think I recognise his boots."

"You *think* you recognise his boots?"

Bull tried not to laugh as I explained what I'd seen and heard in the café.

"Do you think I should report it to the police?"

"Mate, until there are any reports of people going missing or bodies being found the coppers aren't going to be interested."

"But I need to stop him before he kills again. I think he's just been given his next assignment."

"You've been watching too many movies mate. What evidence have you got?"

I silently pondered the fragments of evidence I had.

"What you need is a hair of the dog. Come on, let's go to The Seagull."

Reluctantly, I trudged along the high street feeling like I was having an out-of-body experience. When we arrived at the pub there was only one customer — a young hulk of a man wearing a gorilla costume sitting at a table next to a fruit machine. In front of him sat his mask and a half-finished pint. Busy feeling his flexed bicep beneath the furry sleeve of the outfit, he paid little attention to our arrival.

We ordered a couple of pints before sitting down in a booth next to a pool table, at the far side of the pub, where I continued to explain my concerns.

"Fok me," said Bull looking over my shoulder, "where did you get that from?"

I turned round to see Jim walking towards us wearing an ostrich outfit. A large smile was spread across his face as he used the wire reins to move the bird's head backwards and forwards for comic effect.

"I've just picked it up from the fancy dress shop. It was all they had left."

A small pair of fake legs dangled down from the main body of the costume which was kept in position around his waist by a set of large braces. Flesh coloured tights were stretched over his spindly legs and the outfit was completed by a ludicrous pair of rubber ostrich feet that sat over the top of his trainers.

"Good init?" he said stroking the shimmering tinsel that covered the body of the outfit.

"Where's Micky?" I asked.

"He's had to go looking for another fancy dress shop. Anyway, who wants a drink?"

When he returned from the bar, he squeezed into the booth next to me and I informed him of my dilemma, hoping for some sage advice. His initial concern quickly evaporated when I mentioned the worm incident and I had to concede it may have affected my memory but insisted the episode in the café was real enough.

"What's the plan for today then?" he asked desperate to change the topic.

After a brief discussion, we agreed to go on a pub crawl around the town centre before going to the ball in the evening. Jim clapped his hands.

"Right, that's settled then. Who fancies getting their arse kicked at pool?"

Hoping his ostrich costume would hamper his cue action, I willingly accepted. Bull remained in the booth silently studying the afternoon horse racing.

Once the balls had been racked up, Jim placed the ostriches head on the side of the table and got into position to break off. He drew his cue back as far as he could before thrusting it forward with all the power he could muster. I waited for the pack of balls to explode, but they remained untouched as the white ball flew over the top of them and off the table.

Jim stood up howling with laughter.

"Look at the state of that," he said using his cue as a pointing stick.

Micky walked gingerly across the pub in a skin-tight sexy Santa's helper outfit, complete with stockings, boob tube, PVC mini skirt and long blonde wig.

"It was all they had left," he shouted over the laughter.

The game of pool was quickly abandoned and we returned to the booth where Bull excitedly revealed his tips for the day's horse racing. Jim reached into the body of his outfit and pulled out a fifty-pound note from his wallet.

"Here you are, Micky, go and get us a round of sambucas."

"Blimey, Jim, have you had a winner on the horses?"

He took the note and tottered towards the bar in his high heels. Jim reached back into his wallet and produced three more fifty-pound notes.

"Have a look," he said placing them on the table.

The Queen's head had cleverly been replaced by Mickey Mouse. On the other side was an advert for The Palace nightclub.

Student night every Monday £1 a pint, £1 a shot, £1 entry

"The more you drink, the more you save," said Jim, "and I'm planning on saving my balls off!!"

We all agreed to pay it a visit when we heard raised voices coming from the bar. Micky, with a tray of sambucas in front of him, was having a heated argument with the barman. He examined the *fifty-pound note* that had been thrown back at him then turned to see us laughing and waving the flyers in the air.

"Pay the man, Micky, and damn his impudence," I shouted.

He reluctantly pulled a twenty-pound note from his boob tube.

"You bar-steward," he said when he returned to the table.

"Sorry, Micky, I just couldn't resist it."

Jim looked over, mischievously, at the gorilla in the corner.

"Watch this."

Picking up one of the flyers off the table he gingerly rose from his seat being careful not to knock any drinks over with his outfit.

Moving the ostriches head back and forth with the wire reins he bobbed up and down across the pub. Arriving at the fruit machine next to the gorilla, he pretended to play it for a little while before casually dropping the flyer on the floor, landing it face up. With his mission complete he playfully rode his ostrich back across the pub to rejoin us in the booth. We sat in excited silence waiting for the flyer to be noticed.

Eventually, the young man took a break from admiring his muscles and casually looked around the pub. His eyes swept over the carpet before locking on to the *fifty-pound note*. He looked up and stared directly at us. We immediately looked elsewhere, striking up random conversations with each other, desperate not to give the game away. Stealing fleeting glances in his general direction we fought to hold back fits of the giggles as we subtly elbowed each other in the ribs. Tension rose as we waited for his next move.

He remained seated and we began looking at each other wondering if he had seen it. Then the elbowing started again, as very slowly, a hairy leg appeared from under the table and a rubber gorilla's foot slid silently across the carpet, landing gently on top of the flyer. We tried to suppress our giggles as he calmly reeled in his catch. His hand left the table and headed downwards. Jim let out a shriek. The young man looked up and began to scratch the back of his leg before returning his hand to the table. A few moments passed before he made his next move. Again, his hand left the table and with the finesse of a magician transferred the flyer from under his foot into his pocket.

There was a brief pause before the elbowing started again. We watched as he rose from his seat, ambled across the pub then disappear into the toilets. Moments later he reappeared and we let rip with a chorus of howls, jeers and finger-pointing. Realising it was a prank, he shouted a small selection of swear words, threw the screwed-up flyer at us and stormed out.

We took great pleasure in reliving every moment the poor victim endured until eventually deciding to make our way outside to look for a taxi to take us into town. Spotting a lone one parked at a nearby rank we hurried over, desperate to secure a seat in the back. Experience had taught us whoever got in the front normally ended up paying for the fare. By the time Jim arrived, hampered by his costume, the only seat left was the front one. Reluctantly he gathered up his costume and squeezed in.

*

After a short journey, the taxi arrived in the town centre. The back seat emptied while Jim tried unsuccessfully to palm the driver off with a *fifty-pound note* from his wallet.

"Oh, sorry mate, I didn't realise that was in there," he feebly protested whilst quickly handing over the correct fare.

The Freshers Ball was a big event for first-year students and this one was fancy dress. A sprinkling of students dressed in outfits ranging from monks to superheroes were already noticeable among the normal Saturday afternoon crowd.

The Gander on The Green was the first pub we came across. Strolling past several large motorbikes parked outside we headed inside. If we'd taken the time to read *The Essential Student Guide to Dorset Institute of Higher Education 1989/90* that was given to us on our first day, we would have known this was top of the *Pubs to Avoid* list. The description read 'don't be worried about the big bikes outside, it's the big bikers inside you need to be worried about'. All heads turned as we breezed in blissfully unaware of the honest but unflattering review.

The contrast between us and the hairy bikers was laughable, but nobody was laughing for very different reasons.

My mind was elsewhere as I headed for a gap between two burly bikers at the bar. A busty barmaid approached whilst the larger of the two men, who was wearing a black and white cravat and a thick leather jacket, slowly stroked his steel grey beard as he eyed me up and down. The rest of the lads waited nervously a safe distance away.

"Four pints of Stella please."

Feeling peckish, I leant forward trying to look round the barmaid's heaving chest for any crisps or nuts.

"What sort of nibbles have you got?"

Without warning the two bikers lunged at me and within seconds the whole pub had erupted. Drinks were knocked to the floor as tables overturned. Big bearded men surrounded us, each desperate to land a punch as we were violently manhandled towards the exit.

Within seconds we were back outside in a heap on the pavement. I made a more convincing Rambo now as blood seeped from my nose. The two bikers from the bar towered over us.

The one with the leather jacket was about to put the boot in when the other one pulled him back.

"Leave it, Jez, you don't want another spell inside."

I tried to work out what had sparked this outburst of violence.

"What have we done?"

"Just because my missus has got big tits it doesn't give you the right to ask her what sort of nipples she's got!!"

We remained on the floor as they disappeared back inside the pub. All eyes burned into me as I tried to convince everyone what really happened.

"Honestly, I only asked what sort of *nibbles* she had."

Nursing our cuts and bruises we hauled ourselves off the floor and headed to the next pub.

Fortunately, by the time we reached The Artful Dodger, we had managed to see the funny side.

Two doormen stood on either side of a set of double doors giving us quizzical looks.

"It's ok, it's fake blood," I said pointing at my nose, "it's part of the outfit."

They waved us inside where the atmosphere was buzzing with students wearing a wide variety of fancy dress outfits. I headed straight for the toilets to clean myself up. A quick look in one of the mirrors above the washbasins confirmed I'd only suffered a glancing blow and the blood around my nose looked a lot worse than it was. I bent over to wash the blood off and heard a toilet being flushed in one of the cubicles. When I looked back in the mirror, I was startled to see a large gorilla standing behind me.

"I know you," said an angry muffled voice.

I watched as they removed their gorilla mask.

"You played that *fifty-pound note* prank on me," said the young man from The Seagull as he raised his fist in the air.

"Hang on a minute," I protested, "I had nothing to do with it."

He brought his fist down and prodded me in the chest with a finger.

"You were there laughing at me."

"Yeah, sorry about that. But it was funny."

"I didn't find it funny. Try anything like that again and you'll be getting some of this," he snarled waving his fist.

I watched in silence as he replaced his mask and disappeared back into the pub. After splashing some more water on my face, I went to rejoin the others. They were stood with their backs to the bar admiring the wide variety of costumes on show. Bull handed me a pint.

"You'll never guess who I've just bumped into."

As I told them what happened in the toilet they all began looking around the pub for a gorilla.

"I wouldn't stand for that, Fudge," said Jim, "I'd have knocked him straight out."

"Yeah, right, it's your fault any of this happened in the first place."

"There he is, over there," said Micky gesturing towards some large leather settees arranged haphazardly on the far side of the pub. The gorilla was sat on one of the settees surrounded by several young women dressed as sexy nurses.

"Look at him. Who does he think he is lording it up with all those lovely ladies," said Jim indignantly. "If you let him get away with threatening you now things will only get worse in the future. Go and show him who's boss. If it kicks off, we'll steam in and help you out."

Micky and Bull nervously looked at each other.

Jim continued to goad me, and deep down I knew he was right.

"Come on, Fudge, are you man or mouse?" There was a brief pause before he added, "fetch the cheese."

Something inside of me snapped, and the next thing I knew, I was strolling purposefully across the pub as my friends looked on in stunned silence.

With a short distance to go, I launched into a full-blown verbal assault hoping to stun the ruffian into a groveling apology.

"Oi, you fat, ugly, bastard."

The startled occupants of the settee looked up. A set of confused eyes looked at me from deep inside the gorilla mask.

"Who the fok do you think you are? People like you disgust me."

A few of the nurses began remonstrating, but my focus remained on the big hairy individual who sat conspicuously still in the middle. Sensing my outburst was having the required effect, I continued to attack.

"Why don't you fok off back to where you came from you repulsive creature?"

The hairy shoulders began to jiggle up and down.

"Are you fokkin laughing at me?"

Infuriated, I moved forward and prepared to launch myself at the annoying beast, but an enraged nurse stepped in front of me and began shouting inches from my face.

"What has she done to you?"

I stopped dead. A mixture of emotions washed over me, as well as her hot breath and tiny amounts of phlegm, as she continued her verbal assault.

Surely, I'd misheard. I looked over the nurse's shoulder to see the gorilla had been unmasked to reveal the swollen, watery, makeup-smeared eyes of a plump young lady who was sobbing uncontrollably. The remainder of the nurses tried to console her whilst simultaneously hurling abuse at me.

Bewildered, I turned to my friends who stood a safe distance away solemnly shaking their heads. The irate nurse in front of me took offence to my apparent dismissive behaviour and poked me so hard in the chest that I fell over the back of a settee, landing on top of Robin Hood and Goldilocks, who were equally incensed. Quickly offering my apologies and realising the situation was rapidly spiralling out of control, I hurried back around the settee.

"I'm so sorry. It was a mistake. I thought she was someone else," I blurted, still struggling to compute the speed the pendulum had swung from me being a confident, courageous, seeker of justice to little more than a heartless, aggressive bully.

"I can explain everything. You know The Seagull?"

After a few minutes of non-stop babbling, I felt the mood begin to soften. Most of my grovelling had been directed towards the poor unfortunate soul who'd been the victim of mistaken identity. Feeling overwhelmed with guilt, I signalled to the nurse next to her to make room for me. I sat down and cautiously put my arm over her shoulder. Random strands of black hair clung to her moist round face while lines of makeup streaked from the corners of her eyes. I continued waffling, desperately trying to say something funny that would make her smile or laugh, anything to dissipate the strong sense of sadness which still lingered. Nothing seemed to work, her solemn face stared back at me until eventually, I asked,

"Have you ever had your palm read?"

She looked directly into my eyes and her face morphed from sadness to intrigue.

"Can you read palms?"

"Can I read palms?" I laughed. "Give me your hand."

Tentatively, she held out her hand. It was a big hairy rubber one.

"You'll have to take that off."

I was relieved to hear her chuckle as she took off the gorilla hand and held out her real one. The purple nail varnish was the only clue it may have belonged to a female. Purposefully, I ran a finger over the lines in her sweaty palm, aware of the interest being generated amongst the attractive audience. Turning it one way, then the other, I feigned interest in the various lines that crossed through it, aware that I could soon be holding a much daintier hand and looking into more seductive eyes.

"What's your name?"

"Amy Jones, but my friends call me AJ."

"Well, AJ." I looked up. "Do you mind me calling you AJ?"

She shook her head and I continued to study her hand grateful the first few chapters of *The Beginner's Guide to Palm*

Reading were still fresh in my mind. Gently, I moved my finger along the line that ran across the top of her palm.

"This is your heart line."

Everyone stared intensely, hanging on to my every word.

"Wow," I said, sensing her interest heighten.

"What? What? What is it?"

"Well, I've never seen that before."

It was true. I hadn't seen anything like it before. Her palm was the first one I'd ever read. Softly I tilted her hand one way then the other, trying to utilise the light that was available to examine it closer and add to the mystique.

Eventually, I pointed at two small lines that ran across her heart line.

"These lines, here and here, represent traumatic times in your life."

Tapping the first one, I tried to be as vague as possible, "you lost someone close to you when you were young."

Glancing up, I noticed a fresh tear roll down her cheek.

"And this line is very recent," I said as I continued to tilt her hand.

"Oh no," I paused before taking a gamble, "you've lost someone else, haven't you?"

I looked up to see tears flowing freely down her cheeks and instinctively placed my hand over the top of hers.

"AJ, I'm so sorry."

One of the nurses handed her a tissue whilst another quietly whispered in my ear informing me she'd lost her mum when she was little and her grandma had recently passed away.

Bull appeared behind the settee, shaking his head at the scene in front of him.

"Fudge, we're going to the next pub. Are you coming?"

AJ gave me a slight nod of her head.

"Go on."

"Hopefully, we can continue this another time," I lied before following Bull towards the exit.

"What a plonker," said Jim when we got outside, "I know she was a big girl, but how could you mistake her for that bloke?"

"She had the same gorilla costume on," I protested.

*

We spent the next few hours trying out as many different pubs as we could before making our way to The Freshers Ball.

As we approached the venue, I noticed the bouncers at the entrance looking out for any trouble makers. Back home I'd had plenty of experience of being refused entry into nightclubs and knew that trying to get in as part of a group of drunken lads was not advisable.

"We need to split up. Try and find a bird who's on her own and start chatting to her, at least until we've got past the bouncers. They're less likely to turn you away if they think you're going in with your missus."

Nodding in agreement we all headed off in different directions.

I scanned the area and through the crowds saw AJ's head poking out of her hairy costume. She was walking on her own, clutching her mask. The black streaks down her face had gone but she still looked a pitiful sight. I continued looking, hopeful of spotting someone else but after a fruitless search, my gaze drifted back in her direction. Not wanting to risk being turned away by the bouncers I took a deep breath and reluctantly made my way towards her.

"Hi, AJ, sorry about earlier."

"That's ok. I didn't catch your name."

"Fudge."

"Hi, Fudge."

"Where are your friends, AJ?"

"Oh, they went on ahead of me. I went to get something to eat. I always eat when I'm upset."

"I'm sorry, it's all my fault," I said as I subtly put my arm over her shoulders.

"No, it's not," she kindly protested as we breezed past the bouncers into the main reception area.

A dull thud of music greeted us along with a photographer who directed us to stand in front of an archway of white balloons. He took a quick picture before gesturing towards a set of double doors.

"Would you mind finishing reading my palm?"

"Err, yeah, ok," I hesitated. "Let's go and find somewhere quiet. If we can."

A wall of noise rushed out as we opened the doors to a gigantic auditorium which spread out in all directions in front of us. An impressive domed ceiling rose high above a throng of people on the dance floor some distance away in the centre of the room. The dim lighting only served to heighten our sense of amazement. Different fancy dress outfits cavorted in a cloud of dry ice as laser beams flashed, flickered and whirled around them. Tables and chairs covered in crisp white cotton circled the perimeter where a sprinkling of people were already seated.

At intervals along the walls were bright white neon signs indicating further rooms that lay beyond.

"Over there," AJ shouted and pointed towards a sign which read *Quiet Room.*

The room was intimate, better lit and we could have a conversation without the need to shout. After getting a drink from a small bar area we made our way to an alcove that was recessed into the wall.

Keen to get the reading finished I consoled myself with the notion that it would be good to get some practice before moving on to my intended targets.

Once again, I held her hand and began the charade of reading her palm. It sparkled with a thin film of sweat which helped to highlight the lines as I pondered on what to say next. I recalled what the nurse had whispered in my ear and focused on the first small line that crossed her heart line.

"When I look at this line here, I get an overwhelming sense of sadness. I see a young girl standing by a grave. It's one of your parents."

I looked up to see her large eyes glistening. She nodded slowly.

"It's your mum's grave, isn't it?"

Black streaks once again appeared on her face as she looked at me with her watery eyes and nodded.

"My mum died when I was eight. I remember it like it was yesterday. We were sat at the kitchen table. She was helping me plant a rose seed into a small pot of soil for a school project. Then without a word, she fell from her chair and onto the floor — heart attack."

I could feel my own eyes begin to well up as I continued studying her hand.

"Aww, AJ," I said feeling like a complete charlatan, "and there's been a more recent death in the family."

I drew her hand closer and after feigning intense concentration for a little longer than necessary, I met her moist, expectant gaze.

"It's your grandma."

"Oh, Fudge," her voice faltered.

I put my arm around her.

"Don't be sad, AJ. Your mum and grandma wouldn't want you to be sad. Just focus on all the happy memories you have in here," I said softly touching her head, "and they will always be in here," I continued, as I placed my hand on her heart.

Bull appeared.

"Oh yeah, what's going on here? You two love birds can't leave each other alone."

"No, no. It's not like that," I said quickly removing my hand from AJ's chest.

"Yeah, yeah," he said with raised eyebrows. "Anyway, we're playing a drinking game. Jim and Micky have just bought a bottle of tequila. Are you coming?"

I looked at AJ.

"It's ok, go and enjoy yourself. I need to go and find my friends anyway," she said wiping tears from her eyes.

Racked with guilt, I apologised for upsetting her once again then followed Bull out of the room.

"Blimey, Fudge, first I catch you holding hands and now you're fondling her tits."

My protests were drowned out as he opened the door to the booming auditorium and led me to the *Cocktail Room*.

Inside was an impressive bar area where large mirrors highlighted an extensive array of coloured bottles. Skilled bartenders span bottles in the palms of their hands, above their heads, over their shoulders and occasionally between each other. Some brandished metal cocktail shakers whilst others poured their concoctions into different shaped glasses.

Jim and Micky were sat at a table along with a bottle of tequila, a plate of sliced lemons, a salt cellar and four glasses. Jim looked up.

"Ah, there you are, Fudge. Finally, managed to shake off that gorilla you came in with? What on earth we're you thinking, latching on to that again?"

"She got me in, didn't she?"

"Come on, let's get the game started. All you have to do is repeat what the person next to you says then add your line on the end. If you make a mistake, you have to have a shot of tequila and try again. Understand?"

Having played similar games in the past I nodded confidently and sat down next to him.

I began. "One red hen."

The first round was complete without any mistakes — 'one red hen, two cans of lager, three purple gooseberries, four chocolate ashtrays'.

It was my go again, but before I could finish Jim, Micky and Bull excitedly banged the table shouting, 'down it, down it, down it'.

"You said four chocolate fireguards," Jim laughed.

My face contorted as I downed a shot of tequila and bit into the lemon. I tried again, made the same mistake and downed another tequila. I was successful on my third attempt adding 'five sweaty sailors'.

Bull and Micky managed to repeat it word for word. Jim took a deep breath and started his go.

"One red hen, two cans of lager, three purple gooseberries, four chocolate ashtrays, five sweaty sailors, six barrels of scrumpy, seven fat gorillas…"

He paused briefly to think of the next line to add. A smile spread across his face as he continued, "eight slit sheets, slit by Sam the sheet slitter."

My best attempt was my first. I managed to recite the first seven lines without a problem, but the shrieks around the table soon came when I said "eight shit sleets…"

Twenty minutes later it was still my go. The bottle of tequila was empty. My final effort being, "one chocolate gooseberry."

Chapter Two

I woke up the next morning to the sound of snoring. My eyes flickered open fully expecting to see Bull across the room from me. Thin fabric curtains let in just enough light for me to realise I was in someone else's bedroom. An eerie figure by the door startled me. As my eyes gradually became accustomed to the poorly lit room, I realised it was a gorilla costume.

The snoring continued as I tried to recall the previous night's events. I turned my head slowly on the pillow and through a tangled mess of sweaty hair saw AJ's makeup-smeared face poking out from under the duvet. Looking the other way, I could see my Rambo costume on the floor next to a makeshift bed.

Quietly, I sneaked out a leg from under the duvet and planted my foot softly on the floor.

Next, I slid out an arm and slowly manoeuvred the rest of my body out of the bed. With my eyes fixed on AJ, I silently got dressed.

Taking gentle footsteps across the carpet, I headed towards the closed door, pausing every time a floorboard creaked beneath my feet. With the light touch of a safecracker, I slowly turned the black plastic doorknob. My escape was almost complete, but to my horror, the door didn't open.

Distraught, I twisted the knob as far as it would go and pulled again with more force. It remained closed. In a blind panic, I grabbed the knob with both hands and frantically rattled the door. Still, it wouldn't budge. The snoring stopped and I anxiously looked over my shoulder. The duvet started to move and AJ's face appeared from behind it. Smudged eyes blinked open as she sat up holding the duvet over her chest.

"Where are you going?"

"Erm, I was just, err, going to the toilet. I think the doors locked though."

"No, it's just a bit stiff. Lift the door with the knob as you turn it and then pull."

"Oh, right."

The secret combination worked.

"It's the second door on the right."

Sunlight strained in through old grey net curtains that hung over the windows at either end of the landing. I hurried along a shabby strip of carpet. Desperate to escape I went straight past the second door on the right. At the top of the stairs, I paused and looked down at the thick wooden front door. A small square pane of glass let in just enough light to illuminate a selection of coats that hung above a bulging shoe rack.

Intrigue, guilt, and a full bladder combined to overcome my desire to slip away and I retraced my steps to the toilet. Back at the bedroom door, armed with a feeble excuse to leave, I tentatively pushed it open and was surprised by AJ's outburst.

"Quick, I didn't realise the time, you'll have to go before my dad comes home."

"Your dad!!"

"Yes."

"Is he a student as well?"

"No, you plum. This isn't a student house, it's my home. I've lived here all my life, and if he catches you in my bedroom things could turn ugly."

The duvet was thrown back and a mass of flesh leapt from the bed. A pink fluffy dressing gown was quickly thrown on to cover most of her modesty before I was ushered unceremoniously back across the landing, down the stairs and out through the front door.

Relieved to be outside I reasoned that it was probably best that I couldn't remember the previous night's events.

"Oh, Fudge, are you still ok to help me with my assignment later?"

"Eh?"

"Remember, you promised last night? Please — I really would appreciate it. Will you help me?"

I tried to stop my face from morphing into dismay as I nodded.

"Oh, thank you, meet me in the library at four o'clock."

The door shut and I was left admiring the quaint little cottage that stood before me. The door opened again.

"Go on, quick," she said gesturing up the garden path.

All the way home, I agonised whether to meet her or not. Repeatedly convincing myself one way then the other.

*

It had just gone four o'clock when I walked into the library still trying to remember the night before. A hot shower and normal clothing had helped me feel up to the task. The ground floor was practically deserted, apart from two librarians and someone in a wheelchair studying at one of the many tables dotted about. Upstairs was a handful of people, none of them AJ.

It crossed my mind to leave straight away, but after making the effort I decided to wait for a while. Back downstairs, I grabbed a local newspaper from a pile on reception and settled down at an empty table. The headline simply read — *Missing*.

Images of the harrowing events in the woods, which I'd been happy to blame on the tequila worm, surged back into my mind as I stared at the photo of a smiling girl cuddling a small one-eyed teddy bear. The caption underneath read — *Emily 12yrs old, missing since Friday.*

Out of the corner of my eye, I became aware of the wheelchair user gliding silently towards me. I looked up. My brain struggled to compute what AJ was doing wearing a neck brace and a large plaster cast around her leg.

"What happened?"

"Don't you remember?" she said laughing, "it's part of my Behavioural Studies assignment you plum."

She handed me a clipboard and explained we had to get a bus into town.

"We need to see how wheelchair-friendly Bournemouth is. I need you to make notes of any obstacles we encounter and also observe people's reactions towards me. Come on, let's go."

She wheeled herself towards the exit whilst I quickly tore the front page from the newspaper and put it in my pocket.

Outside, she struggled to get up a slight incline that led to the bus stop so I grabbed the handles at the back of the wheelchair and began to push. Surprised at how hard it was I leant forward to give myself more thrust. With my nose inches from her head, I looked down at her sprawled in the chair with her knitted jumper and grey jogging bottoms and vowed never to overindulge again.

"Quick!!" she said spotting a bus approaching.

I felt like turning the wheelchair around and letting her hurtle back down, but the path had begun to flatten out, and pushing had become a lot easier.

The bus driver rolled his eyes as we appeared alongside him and reluctantly got up to remove a heavy metal ramp from a compartment behind his seat. We watched on as he set about positioning it between the pavement and the bus. After initially struggling with the clunky piece of equipment he managed to get it in place.

"Thank you," said AJ.

"Not a problem," he said unconvincingly before standing aside to allow us to get on board.

Halfway up the steep ramp, I ran out of energy and we both slid gently back down. The bus driver looked at his watch as I made another unsuccessful attempt. I was about to ask AJ to stand up and walk, but a glance at the bus driver dabbing sweat on his forehead with a handkerchief changed my mind. It was too late now for a mini-miracle. After another failed attempt he begrudgingly offered to help. Taking a handle each, we easily managed to get on board with our first effort.

Positioning AJ in the open space in front of the first row of seats I sat down to watch the driver making a show of putting the ramp away.

"Make a note of that, Fudge."

"A note of what?"

"How helpful the driver was."

"Helpful?"

"He helped, didn't he?"

"I suppose."

"Just make a note of it please."

The next stop was outside a pub and having forgotten to put the brakes on the wheelchair it began to move forward as the bus slowed down. I chased after it, but could not stop AJ from careering into the glass doors at the front. A group of revellers waiting at the bus stop took great delight in our misfortune. We ignored them and returned to our original position, making sure the brakes were firmly on.

The mob bundled onboard and I immediately recognised one of them. He wasn't wearing a gorilla suit this time, but jeans and a Dorset Institute of Higher Education rugby top. Our eyes met and he smirked as he came towards me. Instinctively I clenched my fist, but to my surprise, he walked straight past and headed towards the back of the bus. I looked at my reflection in the window and realised how different I looked without my black wig and combat gear.

"Dobbers, can I play on Saturday?" shouted a thin wiry individual who followed him.

"We'll see," he growled.

The rest of the group filed past, each leaving an alcoholic vapour trail. As soon as the bus pulled away offensive comments began to emanate from the back seat.

Adrenaline surged through my body as the remarks about AJ's size, look and condition became more insulting. She sat with watery eyes silently staring through the windscreen. I leant forward and whispered in her ear.

"Do you want me to do something?"

She gave the slightest shake of her head, and I sat back wishing I was a black belt in karate. I pictured myself striding to the back of the bus and effortlessly knocking them all out like I'd seen in the films. I wasn't a black belt, so I didn't.

The journey continued, along with the insults, until we arrived at our stop next to a lush green park. The driver quickly put the ramp in position, but in my haste to get off the bus, I managed to snag the wheelchair on the side of the ramp, causing a wave of jeers to rise up from the back.

"You need to write all this down, Fudge," said AJ tearfully when we eventually got onto the pavement.

Initial relief turned to dread as I realised I'd left the clipboard behind. Back on the bus, the vulgar abuse continued and something inside me snapped.

"Shut up, you bunch of pricks."

Silence descended. Encouraged by the lack of movement, I continued,

"I suppose you think you're all really hard, picking on a poor, vulnerable, young lady. I've got a good mind to kick the shit out of all of you."

To my surprise, they continued to sit in silence, staring at me with open mouths. Feeling my confidence grow, I puffed out my chest, held out my arms and beckoned them towards me with my fingers.

"Come on, who's first?"

Unfortunately, they all wanted to be first. They leapt up and charged towards me.

I span around, ran down the aisle and jumped off the bus.

"AJ, run!!"

Thankfully, the driver, who had witnessed the whole saga, showed some compassion and shut the doors behind me. Fists hammered on the glass. The gang and the bus driver watched in disbelief as AJ miraculously sprang to her feet and sprinted across the park alongside me.

It wasn't long before the emergency exit button was located and the chasing mob bundled out. Shouts from behind alerted us that the chase was back on. We skirted around a small building that housed the public toilets in the centre of the park. I looked round to check if we were out of view. AJ was already lagging behind and breathing heavily. Over her shoulder, I spotted a partially open door at the back of the toilet block.

"Quick, let's hide in there," I said wildly gesticulating at the door.

It was a small store cupboard and we squeezed ourselves in amongst paint pots and gardening equipment. I pulled the door shut plunging us into darkness. A few wisps of light struggled through the small holes in a vent above our heads as we took deep breaths of the acrid air. Pausing moments later, as the sound of thundering feet ran past outside. And only resuming when they had faded into the distance.

"What happened on the bus?" AJ whispered between breaths.

I began to explain but stopped when a soft moaning noise came through the vent. Gingerly standing on a paint pot, I peered into the light of the toilet beyond.

"Can you see anything?"

A man's voice wafted through the vent.

"Oh, Georgio."

Standing on my tiptoes, I peered through the small holes and saw two men passionately kissing each other in the cubicle below. Losing my balance, I put my hand on the wall to steady myself and dislodged a pair of shears that were hanging from a nail. They clattered noisily to the floor. I leaned back into the darkness and stared at the vent.

Slowly, a red and white bandana, that covered the top of a large bulbous head, rose into view along with a rugged, weather-beaten face. The flame of a cigarette lighter was held up to the vent as the man strained to see into the darkness. I reached into my pocket, pulled out a cheap Turkish cigarette, put it in my mouth and leant forward, poking it through the vent and into the flame.

The stranger looked on open-mouthed as I lit the cigarette.

"Cheers, mate," I said out of the side of my mouth.

As soon as I'd uttered the words I began coughing uncontrollably. Losing my footing on the paint pot I tumbled backwards onto AJ and we burst back into daylight landing in a heap outside.

"Quick, we need to go," I said hauling her to her feet.

Retracing our steps, we picked up the plaster casts that had come off during the chase before arriving at the bus stop to retrieve the wheelchair and clipboard.

"What happened back there?" she asked, as I began pushing her back through the park.

"You won't believe this," I said sniggering, "there were a couple of…"

"Uncle Weggy," she shouted.

Gripping the back of the wheelchair, I stared at her uncle's red and white bandana. In the distance, a young, thin, European-looking man walked hurriedly off in the opposite direction.

"AJ, what's happened?" he bellowed.

She laughingly explained about her Behavioural Studies assignment whilst repositioning the plaster cast on her leg.

"This is Fudge, he's very kindly agreed to help me."

My awkward smile quickly gave way to a grimace as I spotted Dobbers and his cronies running towards us.

"Oh, shit."

"I beg your pardon," said Weggy.

Pointing at the approaching mob behind him, I gave a quick explanation of our predicament. Without a word he turned his bulky frame to face them and raised his hand in the air. They came to a shuddering halt just in front of us.

"I take it you've come to apologise for your behaviour on the bus."

Dobbers stood at the front of the pack. His eyes darted wildly between the three of us. Positioning myself behind Weggy, I half smiled as I watched his aggressive demeanour begin to wilt.

"Well?" growled Weggy.

Any lingering thoughts Dobbers may have had of defying the request were soon extinguished when he looked round to see his friends cowering behind him.

"Err," stuttered the ring leader.

"Err, what?"

He looked at the three of us again before his eyes came to rest on AJ.

"Sorry for giving you abuse on the bus."

AJ took the opportunity to berate them all at length. And when Dobbers protested she didn't need the wheelchair, she took great delight in telling him about her assignment.

"And what have you got to say to this gentleman?" said Weggy motioning towards me.

"Erm, sorry for abusing your girlfriend."

"No, she is, err. It's not like that. We're, err, just doing the assignment together," I blurted, whilst shaking my head and waving the clipboard.

I'd gone over the top with my protest and was relieved when Weggy brought the confrontation to a close.

"Go on then, fok off."

Dobbers and his posse begrudgingly turned around and traipsed away. Weggy looked at his watch.

"Well, I'd better be going, darling. Good luck with your assignment."

"Thanks, Uncle Weggy, and thanks for stepping in like that."

"No problem."

Positioning myself back behind the wheelchair I pushed AJ gently through the park.

"It was lucky your uncle showed up when he did."

"Yeah, he just seemed to appear from nowhere. Come on, Fudge, I think we both deserve a drink after all that."

"I couldn't agree more."

The first pub we came across was The Criterion.

There was only one step to negotiate, but it proved to be more difficult than we first thought. To get the smaller front wheels high enough to clear the step the chair had to be tilted right back on the large wheels. Wrestling with AJ's weight I tried to inch the chair forward until the front wheels landed on the step. Once they were in position, I took a few deep breaths then used all my strength to lift the chair on top.

The next problem we faced was the double doors that led into the pub. Reaching over AJ I grabbed the highly polished brass tubular handle of one of the doors and pushed it open whilst using my hips to drive the chair forward. The resistance of an overhead door closer, which sole purpose was to keep the door shut, only served to add to my heightening frustration.

The momentum of the chair came to an abrupt halt as the circular grab rails that protruded from the wheels clattered either side of the opening. It was apparent, both doors would need to be open to get the chair through. AJ leant forward and pushed the other door open creating a large enough gap for us to get in.

"What do you fancy to drink?" I asked, parking AJ next to an empty table.

"I don't mind — surprise me."

Returning from the bar, I placed two pints of cider on the table.

"You really are a prat," she said as I sat down.

"What? I thought it would help quench your thirst."

"No, I'm not on about the drink. Why did you confront those people on the bus?"

"Are you serious?"

"How is this going to look in my assignment? I've got to write a detailed account of what happens. I must give a true reflection of our experiences. Now I've got to include how you lost your temper and tried to incite a fight with those louts."

"They were saying some nasty things about you."

"I know, but you could have got hurt back there."

"Are you honestly going to include the episode on the bus in your assignment? I might end up being incriminated for threatening behaviour."

AJ thought for a while.

"I suppose we could forget to mention that *particular* incident."

"You know it makes sense."

I took a big glug of my drink before asking how she was coping with the recent loss of her grandma. There was a short pause before she responded.

"Not too good, Fudge, to be honest. I feel like I did when my mum passed away," she hesitated, "but this time it seems worse. When my mum died it took me a long time to come to terms with it. The pain never went away I just learnt to live with it. And now my grandma has gone, as well as grieving for her, I feel like I'm grieving for my mum all over again."

I put my arm around her shoulders and gently whispered some kind words of comfort. Tears flowed freely down her cheeks.

"What the devil is going on here?" a man shouted in a posh accent.

I looked up at the irate person standing in front of me. I couldn't decide if the yellow trousers, pink shirt and light green jumper that hung over his shoulders made him look stylish or foolish. On noticing his long dark hair tied back into a ponytail I settled for foolish.

"Well, AJ, what have you got to say for yourself?"

His fierce demeanour softened as he noticed her dewy eyes.

"Awww, babycakes, I'm sorry, I didn't realise you were upset. What's the matter? Is it your gran?"

Removing my arm from around AJ, I got up to allow the stranger to take my place.

"What are you doing here, Hugo?" she croaked.

It soon became apparent this well-spoken individual was her boyfriend, and after a few moments of being ignored, I decided to leave them alone.

Outside, I ambled along the pavement, smiling at the assumption I'd made about the previous night. I'd taken it for granted I'd been lured back and hadn't thought to ask AJ what had actually happened. The makeshift bed on the floor now made sense as I blamed the alcohol for any amorous advances I might have made during the night.

After a few ponderous miles, my attention was drawn to The Seagull. Sounds from the jukebox accompanied the hum of chatter that emanated through the frosted glass windows. I walked past but soon came to a laboured stop. After a few moments of deliberation, I turned around and wandered in.

Looking around for familiar faces I was pleased to see Bull sat in a booth swigging back the last few drops of his drink while his eyes remained fixed on the sports section of the newspaper in front of him.

"Alright, Bull."

"Fudgcy, where've you been?"

"Do you want another one?" I said gesturing at his empty pint glass.

"Does the pope shit in the woods?"

"Fok me, how many have you had?"

Bull smiled and after getting two fresh pints I settled down opposite him.

"You know you said don't go to the police until there's a report of someone going missing."

"Yeah."

"Well take a look at this," I said dramatically slapping the newspaper article on the table.

He grabbed the scrap of paper and began to read it. After a few expletives, he looked up.

"What are you going to do?"

"I don't know mate. I had convinced myself I'd imagined what happened in the woods."

"The trouble is, Fudge, now this has come to light, I think you've got no choice but to let the police know. At least your conscience will be clear."

"But what if that worm did cause me to hallucinate?"

Bull tapped his finger on the paper.

"It says here you can phone anonymously with any information, no matter how insignificant it might seem." He paused and looked me in the eye, "you need to let them know."

The dramatic sensation was fleeting as he suddenly clapped his hands.

"Anyway, do you fancy a couple of tequilas?"

I winced as if I'd just bitten into a slice of lemon.

"Good lad," he said and headed for the bar.

The little girl's face stared back at me from the article in the paper. I picked it up and looked at the phone number.

As I agonised whether to call I casually turned the piece of paper over. On the other side was a competition to win one thousand pounds. It was a welcome distraction to fantasise about how I would spend it. A mystery man was going to be in town the following week. If you recognised him you had to show him the picture and say 'I know it's you, you're Mr Blue' and he would give you one thousand pounds cash. There was a blurry picture of a man's face, only his eyes and eyebrows were in focus. My mind wandered at the thought of winning the money. It was clear my grant cheque wouldn't stretch until the end of term and getting a part-time job seemed the only realistic option.

My daydream was cut short when Bull placed a tray of shots in front of me complete with lemon wedges and a salt cellar.

"So, are you going to speak to the police?" he asked sprinkling salt on the back of his hand.

"I suppose so, but how can I be sure I'll remain anonymous? I don't want to be the killer's next victim."

Bull licked the salt from his hand, downed a shot of tequila and bit down on a piece of lemon. This sudden flurry of activity seemed to give him the answer.

"Use the public payphone at the end of the bar. They won't be able to trace you. You'll feel better once you've got it off your chest then you can forget about it."

After a few shots of tequila, I plucked up enough courage to make my way over to the payphone. Tentatively picking up the receiver I looked around to make sure nobody was in earshot then dialled the number.

A woman answered and I began to blurt out what I'd seen in the woods.

"Slow down, slow down. What did this man look like?"

I could hear the disappointment in her voice as I explained how my visibility had been obscured. She perked up briefly as I went on to describe what happened in the café.

"I think it might have been the same man. He was certainly wearing similar boots."

"He was wearing *similar boots*?" she baulked, doing little to hide the sarcasm in her voice.

Trying to bolster my story I began telling her about the scratches on his arms but stopped mid-sentence when I noticed a shifty-looking man lurking behind me. Still gripping the receiver, I turned to face the bar. Through the earpiece, I could hear the woman on the other end enquiring if I was still there. Without a word, I put the receiver back and returned to my seat.

Sitting down, I looked towards the payphone. The man had gone.

"Did you tell them everything?" asked Bull.

"Kind of," I said, nervously scanning the rest of the pub, but the man was nowhere to be seen.

Bull assured me I had done the right thing, but all I could think about was the shifty-looking man. I picked my pint up and downed it in one go.

"Blimey, Fudge, have you got a train to catch?"

"No, mate, I'm a bit tired. I'm going to get a takeaway and go home."

"What about the rest of these shots?"

"You drink them."

"Ok, matey, I won't be late, we're cooking in the student kitchens tomorrow."

Back outside, it wasn't long before I came across the large, brightly lit, blue and white sign of The Momtaz Indian Restaurant. There were two signs in the window, *Takeaway Available* and *Staff Wanted – Apply Within*.

Warm spicy aromas floated pleasantly out of the door as soon as I opened it. Inside, the restaurant was a bustling hive of activity. Over at a small bar area, I began to study a laminated takeaway menu that was stuck to the top of the counter with sticky tape. An Asian man in black trousers, white shirt and black bow tie lingered in front of me. Feeling adventurous I thought I might try something different instead of my usual chicken dhansak and pilau rice. Taking my time to read the brief description next to every dish, I came up with a shortlist. As I whittled my final selections down further, the man behind the counter became increasingly impatient.

"Sir, your order please!!"

I panicked.

"Chicken dhansak and pilau rice please."

Whilst at the bar, a steady flow of waiters came to get drinks for the tables they were serving. Chatting to one of the friendlier ones, I told him about the catering course I was doing.

"You should apply for the job in the kitchen."

I couldn't help but laugh.

"No, seriously. How many students would be able to put they've worked in an Indian restaurant on their CV?"

"I suppose you've got a point."

"And you get a free curry to take home at the end of the night," the waiter added.

Before long I was speaking to the manager arranging a trial shift for the following evening.

"I promise I won't let you down," I said shaking his hand.

Back on the high street I strolled home merrily swinging my bag of curry and rice. But before I could begin to feel too pleased with myself about securing a job the still night air was pierced by a crescendo of wailing sirens. Police cars and vans sped past with their flashing blue lights bouncing off shop windows as they went.

I watched the lights flutter into the distance before disappearing in the direction of the woods. Intrigue got the better of me and I decided to take a detour. The sound of dogs barking echoed in the distance and the atmosphere grew more sinister as I got closer. Bright lights flickered out through the trees whilst blue lights intermittently lit up the forest from the outside. Flimsy blue and white police tape had already been wrapped around the perimeter masquerading as an impenetrable barrier.

Through the trees, several police officers wearing high visibility jackets wrestled to hold back frantically yapping dogs as torches shone haphazardly in the undergrowth. If there was a body in there, I wanted it to be found.

Two uniformed policemen were being quizzed by a small crowd as they guarded one of the entrances. Making my way to the fringes of the group I listened to the various theories that were being discussed. With the police officers refusing to disclose any information, most assumed they were searching for the missing girl and begged to be allowed in to help. Others seemed content just watching the drama unfold. Not wanting to get drawn into any speculation I headed home unaware of the shifty-looking man from the pub quietly staring at me from a distance.

*

Back home, I soon gave up my search for a clean plate and began looking for one covered in the least amount of grime. I found a badly chipped black one with only a mild smearing of tomato sauce on it. After giving it a quick wipe with a soggy dishcloth, I tipped my food on and went to look for a spoon. Faced with an empty cutlery draw, I was forced to nervously plunge my hand into the murky cold water of the sink. After a few attempts, I brought one to the surface and gave it a quick swill under the tap.

Deep in thought, I sat down at the table. My appetite had gone by now and after only managing to eat one mouthful, I reluctantly pushed away the plate and went to bed.

Settling down under the warmth of my duvet I tried to go to sleep, but the faint sound of dogs barking drifted through the open window, acting as a constant reminder of the macabre situation unfolding nearby.

Recent events replayed over and over until eventually, I slipped into an uneasy sleep.

Soon, I was back in the woods, crouching behind a bush, staring at the same boots. But this time, I did step on a twig. The snap was deafening, and I found myself looking into the blood-red eyes of a hideous creature. It lunged at me through the undergrowth. Leaping to my feet, I began sprinting through the trees as the sound of wild screeching noises and thunderous footsteps chased after me.

Bursting out of the woods into daylight, I fell to the ground gasping for breath. With all my energy sapped, I stared helplessly back at the tree line and waited for the beast to emerge, but the forest fell silent. Drained of all my energy, I lay back and shut my eyes. The faint sound of dogs barking floated in the air. I opened my eyes and stared into the darkness of my bedroom.

Chapter Three

The following morning, I was woken by Bulls radio alarm and immediately recalled the terrifying dream. Looking across the room I felt reassured to see him stirring in his bed. The badly chipped black plate lay empty on the floor next to him.

"Bull, Bull, wake up."

His eyes flickered open, and I told him what I'd seen on the way home.

"Blimey, they don't hang about. I wonder if they've found anything," he said turning the volume up on his radio as a news bulletin began.

The newsreader reported that after an anonymous tip-off the police had begun searching the woods, but so far nothing had been found. We looked at each other in silence as the missing girl's mother made an emotional plea for her daughter to return home and for anyone with information to ring the helpline. The newsreader went on to say that the police wanted to make an urgent appeal to the person who rang up anonymously as the call had seemingly been cut short before all the information had been gathered.

"I thought you'd told them everything."

I explained about the man in the pub who appeared to be listening in on my phone call.

"I couldn't risk it, Bull. Do me a favour and don't tell anyone I rang up. I don't want a single person finding out it was me who tipped off the police."

"My lips are sealed, but you'd better ring them back and finish off that phone call."

"Ok, ok," I said reluctantly.

Bull glanced at the time on his alarm clock.

"Come on, we better get a move on, we've got mouths to feed."

"Talking of mouths to feed, I see you helped yourself to my curry," I said motioning towards the plate.

"Sorry mate, when I got back it was just there — all alone — on the kitchen table — begging to be eaten."

"Yeah, I lost my appetite after seeing all the commotion in the woods, but I'm starving now."

"I'm sure they'll be plenty of opportunities to get something to eat in our Food and Beverage practical lesson later."

The student kitchen provided cut-price dishes for The Thomas Hardy Restaurant which was open to the public allowing students to practice their cooking and waiting skills in a real-life setting.

We hurriedly got ready and after finding Jim and Micky's bedrooms empty made our way to campus.

*

Arriving late we found the small changing room deserted and quickly put on our chef's whites. The door burst open and in rushed a flustered Micky.

"Are you ok?" I asked.

"No, I'm not — me and Jim ended up at a house party last night and I woke up about half an hour ago on someone's settee. Jim was nowhere to be seen. Now I'm late for Front of House and to make matters worse I've forgotten my waiter's uniform."

He headed straight for the lost property basket and began throwing various items of clothing over his shoulder, eventually finding a pair of trousers that were a few sizes too small and a crumpled up white shirt. Desperate not to miss his first session in the restaurant he set about squeezing into the trousers. There was an almighty racket as he hopped around banging into the metal lockers trying to get his legs in. He inched them up towards his boxer shorts until eventually, he was able to mount an attempt at doing them up. His face contorted as he strained to bring the button closer to the hole. After a few failed attempts he lay on the floor hoping to make it easier. We offered our assistance. As he breathed in, we tried to button him up but were still a few millimetres short.

"It's no good. You'll have to take your boxer shorts off," I joked.

Despite our protests, he whipped them off and pleaded with us to try again.

We reluctantly crouched over him and tried to wrestle his trousers over his exposed genitals. The door crashed open and in burst our tutor who'd heard the commotion from the kitchen below. He was a short stocky man who looked extremely irate in his pristine chef's whites.

"What the fok is going on here?"

His sleeves were rolled up exposing an array of tattoos on his forearms. It was clear he was ex-military. Sensing imminent danger, we leapt to our feet and quickly explained ourselves. Even with Micky backing up our story he seemed reluctant to believe us. It was clear he had hoped to give us a good kicking as he stood with his chest heaving in and out.

After pausing to consider the plausibility of our account of events he begrudgingly said, "just hurry up and get downstairs."

Micky lay back down and after a few more attempts we managed to do his trousers up and help him to his feet.

"Can you walk in them?" I asked.

The restricted movement had the effect of making him look very effeminate as he struggled to walk up and down the changing room.

"They'll have to do," he said putting his shirt on.

"I need a bow tie as well."

An abandoned one was found collecting dust on top of the lockers which completed his dishevelled look.

"I don't know which outfit's worse, Micky, this one or Santa's helper."

He rolled his eyes and gingerly headed off to the restaurant for silver service training whilst we made our way to the kitchen.

The man who came close to launching an all-out attack on us moments earlier now stood calmly next to a square stainless-steel table in the centre of a large, bright, squeaky-clean kitchen. He was showing an audience of fresh-faced students how to prepare a dish from the day's menu. They were all stood in their brand-new chef's whites like scientists watching an experiment, marvelling at the culinary skills that were on show. Without the slightest glimmer of acknowledgement of our arrival, he continued with his demonstration. Each item of food was arranged on the plate with great care and when any rogue specks dared to venture onto the rim, he reached for the cloth that was draped over his shoulder and wiped them away.

"Remember guys, you eat with your eyes," he kept saying as he finished each dish by adding a sprig of parsley then sliding the plate into the centre of the table for everyone to admire.

On completion of the last demonstration, he handed out recipe cards with instructions on how to prepare each specific dish. Bull and I were the last to receive them.

"You two are in charge of the chicken noodle soup and beef with rice. Your work stations are over there, next to the serving area."

As he walked off, he gestured towards a white thickset door with a large metal handle.

"You'll find everything you need in there."

We studied the cards for a few moments before going in search of the required ingredients. Behind the sturdy door was a large storage area that was heavily stocked with the vibrant colours of fresh fruit and vegetables. Two further doors inside revealed a room full of great fleshy cuts of meat and another room full of delicious cakes and desserts. All very different from our kitchen which housed the sum total of a handful of frozen peas screwed up in a bag at the back of the freezer. All thoughts of why we were there evaporated as we began to scan every rack, shelf and draw to see which goodies we could take back home. But with other students milling around we could only get the ingredients required for our designated dishes.

Back out in the kitchen, I unravelled my brand-new set of knives from the cream hessian cloth they came in. The tutor must have sensed danger as he reappeared to give me a crash course on how to use them correctly. Holding on to a carrot with his fingernails pointing inwards he pressed the side of the knife against his knuckles, keeping the tip of the blade on the chopping board. We watched mesmerised as the once intact root vegetable turned into a pile of dice-sized pieces within seconds. The chicken was next. He rotated the dead bird around on the chopping board as if it was on a potter's wheel — rhythmically pausing to make precise incisions until the meat had been completely stripped from the bone. For his finale, he twirled the knife around in his hand before slamming the blade down hard into the carcass. He stared at the pair of us, almost daring us to say something, before slowly releasing his grip on the handle.

"Use that to make the stock for the soup. Any questions, I'll be in my office."

We didn't know whether to be impressed or frightened.

"He could've sliced the beef as well the lazy bar-steward," Bull joked as he tugged the knife free and began slicing the chicken into thin strips.

I chopped the remaining vegetables and gently fried them along with the chicken. After putting them into a large pot to simmer, I casually wandered over to the double doors that led into the restaurant and looked through a glass porthole. Micky moved cautiously around a table as he practised his silver service skills. A smile crept across my face as I watched him chase a bread roll around a silver platter with a large fork and spoon.

Soon the first customers began to arrive. A small machine at the end of the stainless-steel serving area whirred into life printing the first order of the day.

The tutor emerged from his office and clapped his hands.

"Right guys, it's showtime."

Tearing off the slip of paper he boomed, "two soup, one beef, one scampi."

I ladled some soup into a couple of bowls as a sizzling noise broke out behind me.

"What are you doing?" the tutor shouted at Bull who had started cooking a portion of beef in a large wok, "they haven't had their soup yet."

Bull sheepishly fished the beef out of the hot oil as I placed tiny sprigs of parsley on top of the soup and put them under the bright lights of the hot plate. The doors to the restaurant swung open and Micky came in like a gunslinger entering a saloon after spending two days in the saddle.

"What's the matter?" I asked.

"I think these trousers are cutting off the circulation to my legs."

"They look like they've been sprayed on. Any tighter and I'll be able to tell what religion you are."

He was in no mood for jokes as he picked up the soups and walked robotically back into the restaurant.

A few more soups later and I began to get concerned with the ever-expanding noodles in the pot.

"Hey, Bull, did you put the right amount of noodles in here."

"Yeah, two hundred ounces."

"Two hundred ounces!! It was supposed to be twenty ounces!! No wonder all the soup is disappearing."

I managed to dish out a few more portions by plunging the ladle deep into the noodles and scooping out the remaining liquid.

Micky shuffled back through the doors.

"How much soup is left?"

"Why?"

"A table of six has just come in and they all want soup."

"Shit. I'll see what I can do."

He went back to serve them bread rolls using his newfound silver service skills. Moments later, raucous laughter and jeering came through the double doors, quickly followed by Micky with a panicked look etched on his face.

"What's happened?"

"I dropped a roll on the floor and these trousers are so tight when I bent down to pick it up, they split open."

He turned round to reveal his exposed arse crack.

In an attempt to hide it, I tucked a tea towel into the back of his trousers and sent him out with six bowls of noodles. Shortly afterwards, the doors to the restaurant flew open. Micky hurried back in as a roll flew past his ear landing at my feet.

"What's going on?"

"They're not happy. They wanted soup, not noodles. They're getting very angry. They want to skip straight to the main course. We need to get them served quickly and out of here before things get ugly."

I turned to Bull.

"How long for six beef and rice?

"There's a slight problem," he said shamefaced, "I've run out of rice."

"What? Can't you cook some more?"

"It will take too long. We'll have to give them noodles instead."

"Oh, goodie."

Shaking my head, I ladled out six piles of noodles next to the beef and put the plates on a large tray ready to be sent out.

"Wait, wait, wait," shouted Bull hurrying over.

I looked around, hoping he'd found some more rice.

"Remember, you eat with your eyes," he said placing small sprigs of parsley on top of the noodles.

Micky picked up the tray, took a deep breath and walked uncomfortably back to the table. Another commotion soon erupted in the restaurant. I went to look through the porthole, but before I could get there Micky burst back through the doors covered in noodles.

"It's all kicking off out there."

The riotous noise grew louder as I continued cautiously towards the doors. A handful of noodles splattered on the porthole and slowly slid down. Bull appeared next to me and we both peered through the smudged glass at the wild scene beyond. A food fight had broken out between the table of six. They were hurling noodles, bread rolls and beef at each other. The restaurant had emptied of all other customers. Waiters and waitresses cowered behind the bar.

"I'll go and get the tutor," Bull said.

The situation looked like it was going to get even worse as I noticed one of the party about to hurl a plate at the bar. Recognising the troublemaker, I flung open the doors.

"Dobbers! Put that fokkin plate down!" I said with as much authority as I could muster.

Stopping mid-throw, it took him a few seconds to realise who was standing in the doorway wearing crisp chef's whites.

"Not you again."

"Yeah, me again. Put that plate down and get the fok out of here."

"And what are you going to do if I don't."

"Me? Nothing, but we both know someone who might."

The rest of the gang had stopped throwing things and watched silently as Dobbers reluctantly put the plate back on the table.

"Come on, lads, let's get out of here."

With my heart pounding, I watched them file out of the restaurant. When the last one had left, I turned to the row of heads behind the bar.

"It's ok, you can come out now."

They all slowly rose to their feet. I smiled at a slender young waitress with strawberry blonde hair tied back in a bun and made my way back into the kitchen. Bull and the tutor emerged from his office.

"What's going on?" he growled.

"Oh, just a few troublemakers. They've gone now."

He held open the doors to the restaurant and surveyed the relatively calm aftermath. The waiting staff fussed around the table clearing up all evidence of the disturbance. The tutor, visibly disappointed to have missed an opportunity to administer his unforgiving brand of retribution, stepped back into the kitchen and looked at his watch

"Right guys, that's a wrap. Lunchtime is over. Well done everyone."

After a quick clean of our workstation, we headed back to the changing rooms, where Micky was already lying on his back trying to peel off his trousers. When he'd finished, he stood up, naked from the waist down, and slung the trousers in the direction of the lost property basket.

"Fok me, Fudge, you showed some balls in that restaurant."

"Well, you're showing some in the changing rooms. Do you mind covering them up?"

"Oh yeah," he said hopping into his boxer shorts, "I thought you were going to get a kicking out there. Come on, you deserve a pint in the student union bar."

"I can't matey, I've got to work later."

"I'm paying."

"Ok, just a quick one."

The bar was the size of a small warehouse. A cavernous, open plan room with a spacious wooden floor that spread out towards the long bar opposite. To the right, a row of oversized windows let in vast amounts of daylight whilst a huge stage lay dormant to the left.

"Three pints of lager please," Micky said to the barman.

"You better make that four."

We all turned round to see Jim striding towards us.

"Where have you been?" I asked.

"Oh, I ended up going back to some bird's house after the party. Anyway, who fancies going to The Palace tonight?" he said waving a handful of flyers in the air.

Bull and Micky excitedly agreed to go. I couldn't help but look despondent.

"I can't mate, I'm working at The Momtaz tonight."

I looked at Jim and waited for a wisecrack, but he was too busy ogling the sultry young lady wearing a waitress's outfit that had appeared next to me. Her long, strawberry blonde hair had been released from the bun and now flowed freely over her shoulders.

"This is for you," she said handing me a pint.

"Sorry, but I didn't order one."

"I know you didn't. I've bought it for you."

"Why?"

"For what you did in the restaurant."

"Oh, it was nothing, they were bang out of order. Especially the big one, what a twat. He was lucky I didn't do my karate moves on him," I said making a chopping motion with my hand.

"That *twat* is my boyfriend," she replied somewhat embarrassed.

"What? You're joking."

"No, he's lovely really, but once he's had a drink he turns into a bit of a wally."

"A bit of a wally!!" I said as all amorous thoughts quickly vaporised. "What's your name?"

"Bev."

"Well, thank you, Bev, that's very kind of you."

"You're welcome," she smiled.

We all watched mesmerised by the hypnotic movement of her buttocks as she walked back across the wooden floor towards the exit.

"Wow, it looks like her arse is chewing a toffee," said Jim.

I waited until she'd disappeared from view before turning back around.

"Can you believe it? A stunner like that going out with that twat?"

"Yeah, some people get all the luck," replied Micky shaking his head.

"Fudge, you are something else, 'he was lucky I didn't do my karate moves on him', I'd like to have seen that," Bull laughed.

As the afternoon wore on, they all took turns to try and persuade me to ring in sick for my first shift. But the fact I'd promised the manager I wouldn't let him down and the thought of a free curry eventually made me leave and honour my obligation.

*

The Momtaz looked different in the early evening light, blending in with all the other shop fronts on the high street. I walked past it at first, but the spicy aromas soon alerted me to its proximity.

The neon *open* sign was switched off and the door was locked. Peering through the window I could see a waiter setting up the tables inside. A gentle tap on the glass failed to catch his attention so I began hammering with my fist. The waiter looked up and nonchalantly pointed at his watch.

"Six o'clock," he mouthed, holding up six fingers for extra confirmation.

"I'm here to work."

A brief conversation went back and forth accompanied by some animated sign language. The glass did its best to muffle the conversation between us until eventually the waiter came over and opened the door.

"We don't open until six o'clock," he said indignantly.

"I don't want to eat. I'm here to work."

Trying to convince the disbelieving man, I opened up my bag and showed him my chef's whites and knives.

Someone shouted in a foreign language behind him. I was relieved to see the manager standing in a doorway at the back of the restaurant. There was a further volley of foreign words before the waiter stepped aside and ushered me in.

Previous experiences of Indian restaurants, as a customer, had always been enjoyable. Now I was there to work, an uneasy feeling rose as I threaded my way through the empty tables.

"You made it then," said the manager with an air of disappointment.

The kitchen was a lot smaller than I'd imagined and was in sharp contrast to the bright sanitised one I'd worked in earlier. The heat and intense aromas took me by surprise. The head chef came over and exchanged a few words with the manager before rolling his eyes and walking off.

"Follow him," the manager said.

I was led past a couple of kitchen staff wearing heavily stained uniforms who barely acknowledged me. We stopped next to a big sack of red chillies. The head chef took a knife from a nearby chopping board and a single chilli from the sack. He briefly held the chilli in the air before proceeding to thinly slice it, scoop it up with the blade of the knife and put it in a large metal bowl. Using the knife, he pointed to the sack of chillies, followed by the chopping board and finally the bowl.

"Come and see me when you're done," he said in broken English.

"Where can I change?" I said showing him the contents of my bag.

He put the knife down and I followed him towards a door with a flimsy metal toilet sign on it. The man smiled exposing a row of dark yellow teeth as he opened the door with one hand and pointed inside with the other, bowing down as if it was the entrance to a grand palace.

"In here."

The two kitchen staff behind me sniggered as I peered inside. It was crammed with all manner of foodstuff. I assumed the sign on the door was a joke until I noticed part of a porcelain toilet underneath bags of onions, tins of spices and jars of pickles. It was clear the toilet had been out of action for a while as the bowl itself now housed a large bag of potatoes. The man leant past me and pulled a cord that hung down over a drum of cooking oil. A lone bulb above his head came on.

Faced with no other alternative, I squeezed inside, pulled the door shut and got changed as quickly as the cramped space would allow.

Back at my designated area of the kitchen, I placed a handful of chillies on the chopping board and began to slice them using my recently learned knife skills. The first orders soon started coming in from the restaurant. Large frying pans sizzled into life accompanied by the rhythmical tinny sound of long metal spoons that tossed and turned the delicious smelling contents over the intense heat of gas flames.

The kitchen filled with more staff members and the noise level rose as they talked to one another in their native tongue. I felt like I was in a kitchen in a faraway land. The heat and aromas added to the surreal experience. Unsure if I was the topic of conversation I drifted into a world of my own, pondering on recent events. The heart-wrenching plea of the little girl's mother replayed over and over as I monotonously cut the chillies.

The earlier drinking session meant the need to visit the toilet crept quickly upon me. Hurriedly, I finished chopping the remaining chillies before proudly informing the head chef. He did not attempt to hide his disappointment at my shoddy culinary skills, but I didn't have time to take offence. I had more pressing matters to attend to.

"I need to go to the toilet," I said pointing at the makeshift changing room.

"No, not that one, you'll have to use the one in the restaurant."

It was alive with customers. Waiters, dotted around the room, served delicious smelling food from small wooden trollies. Whilst making my way to the toilet I glanced over at a couple sitting in the corner of the room. My eyes darted back. Hugo and a smartly dressed young lady were leaning over their meals, locked in a long lingering kiss. On the end of the table was an ice bucket complete with an open bottle of champagne. After uncoupling their lips, they clinked their glasses together. As Hugo took a sip, he looked up at me and immediately spat champagne back into his glass.

Putting my head down, I hurried to the toilet. The relief of arriving in front of the urinal was short-lived. I became aware of an acute tingling sensation in my manhood which very quickly turned into intense burning pain. On looking down I realised the chilli juice which covered my fingers was responsible. The soft skin which I held in my hands was defenceless as the pain soared to dizzying heights.

In a panic, I let go. Urine sprayed across the floor as I staggered towards the washbasins. Cocking my leg up I ran the cold tap and began frantically splashing water trying to relieve the agony.

My head began to spin and there was a bright flash.

I looked into the large mirror in front of me and saw Hugo standing in the doorway holding a small camera. We both stared at my sorry reflection in the most unnatural of poses.

With tears of pain in my eyes, I tried to explain what I was doing whilst continuing to splash water over my genitals.

Hugo smiled and shook his head.

"Well, well, this is embarrassing — but if you don't tell anyone you've seen me, I won't show anyone the photo," he said holding up the camera and gently shaking it. Vulnerable and desperate, I nodded.

"There's a good boy," he said as I watched him return to the restaurant.

Not wanting the embarrassment of explaining myself to anyone else, I quickly uncocked my leg from the basin and did my trousers back up.

The stinging sensation was still excruciating as I tentatively made my way back to the kitchen to inform the manager of my predicament.

He found it hard to grasp my explanation. Tears ran freely down my face as I gesticulated wildly at the chillies and my nether regions. In the end, I gave up.

"My cock is on fire. I quit."

My request for a free curry was met with a few choice swear words as was my demand for payment for the short time I'd been there.

Desperate to leave the premises I quickly got changed and made my way out through the restaurant resisting the temptation to look over at Hugo. Who I knew would be sat there staring at me with a smug grin on his punchable face.

Taking deep breaths of the cool evening air I was relieved to feel the pain gradually rescind as I walked home. I wondered how AJ would react if she knew about Hugo and his dinner date. Of course, he would deny everything and persuade her that it was a pathetic attempt on my part to split them up. I pictured Hugo as he convinced her that I was just jealous of their perfect relationship.

Arriving home, I opened the front door.

"Mr Fudge?"

Startled, I span around and was confronted by the shifty-looking man from the pub. My mind raced. Should I run? Should I try and get in the house? Should I shout for help?

"Mr Fudge," he repeated, "we were hoping that you would call us back."

My look of confusion prompted him to show me his ID badge.

"Detective Inspector Cashun — I need to speak with you down at the station."

"What about?"

"I think you know exactly what about. I've had to deal with a lot of anonymous phone calls over the years, but I'm not normally standing next to the person when they make them. I followed you back home last night."

"Oh."

"I've been waiting for you to ring back with the rest of the details."

"Yeah, sorry, I err…"

"I'm not sure you grasp the seriousness of this case. A young girl has gone missing and so far you are the only person who has come forward with any information. I feel partly responsible because I know you cut your phone call short when you noticed me."

I nodded.

"Yeah, I was going to say that the following morning I went for breakfast at the Halloween Café and…"

DI Cashun raised his hand.

"We need to talk about this down at the station."

"Ok."

I put my knives and chef's whites inside the house and shut the front door as he signalled to a car further down the road. Bright headlights came on and it slowly pulled up alongside us.

The driver, a plain-clothed officer, made no effort to acknowledge my arrival on the back seat.

"Let's go," said the detective as he got into the passenger seat.

Mysterious voices crackled intermittently from a police radio as I breathed in the pungent smells that emanated from inside the car. As we sped through the streets, I wondered how many previous occupants had been chauffeured to the police station. And like most of them, wished I was somewhere else. Namely, in amongst the swaths of revellers that were merrily making their way towards town for a night out.

The police station was a very unflattering building. Once inside, I followed DI Cashun through a short network of drab corridors. We came to a stop and he opened a door marked *Interview Room 1.*

"Take a seat. I'll be back in a minute."

The room was cold and grey. A small piece of equipment, which I assumed was a recording device, sat on top of a table in the middle of the room. Four plastic chairs were scattered around it. Slumping into one of them I gazed at the sparse surroundings wandering how much help I would be to the investigation. DI Cashun entered the room holding a thick paper folder with *Emily Williams – Missing* written on the front.

"Once again, Mr Fudge, I'm sorry I had to bring you here, but these are unprecedented circumstances."

He sat down opposite and thudded the folder on the table.

"I recently met with the missing girl's mother, who, as you can imagine, is inconsolable right now. It doesn't help that the last time she saw her daughter they'd argued. And as for her father..."

He stopped and looked at me.

"What about her father?"

"He's a well-known gangster. The sort you don't want to get on the wrong side of. You must tell me every little detail before anyone else gets hurt."

He pressed some buttons on the machine in front of him and formally began the interview.

The natural starting point seemed like the party. DI Cashun eagerly began to make notes but put his pen down the moment I mentioned the hallucinogenic worm.

"So, let me get this straight, you had a hallucinogenic worm just before you walked back home through the woods?"

"Yes."

"You didn't mention this when you rang up."

"I didn't think it was relevant at the time," I said indignantly. "Look, I know what you're thinking, but I can assure you, what I saw in the woods felt real enough."

The detective rubbed his face with his hands and let out a long sigh.

"Ok, tell me what happened in the woods," he said picking his pen back up.

I explained about the metallic screech that first alerted me to someone's presence and the subsequent appearance of the eerie individual. DI Cashun half-heartedly made notes until the point where the man disappeared out of my view.

"How tall would you say this man was?"

"It's difficult. I was crouched down and didn't get a good look at him."

"If you had to guess."

"About average height."

"And what is average height?"

"I don't know, about five foot ten inches."

"Right, Mr Fudge, so we're looking for a man about five foot ten inches, who wears black boots with buckle straps, a trench coat and smokes? That's not a lot to go on."

"And he's got a new spade," I said hopefully.

"I doubt very much, Mr Fudge, that he'll still be wandering about carrying his new spade."

"I've got a feeling, I might have seen the same man in a café the following morning."

The detective perked up. However, his face soon dropped as I began to explain about the chance encounter.

"So, apart from the boots looking familiar, there was nothing else to suggest it was the same man from the woods?"

"Well, he had scratches on his arms."

He looked at me quizzically.

"They might account for the blood I saw."

"Maybe — and what about the man he was talking to, can you describe what he looked like?"

"Not really, I only saw him from behind."

Another look of resignation, but I persevered and went on to describe the angel wings tattoo on the back of his head. The detective was visibly disappointed as he scribbled down a few more notes before concluding the interview.

"Look, Mr Fudge, I'm sure you had the greatest intentions of helping us with our inquiries, but we can't put out a photofit of a pair of old boots. I'll pay a visit to the," he paused as he looked back through his notes, "Halloween Café and see if anyone knows who these men are."

"Please don't mention anything about me."

"Don't worry, Mr Fudge, you'll remain anonymous," he said reaching into his pocket.

"Here, take my card. If you remember anything else give me a call."

The detective led me back down the corridors to the exit where I declined his offer of a lift home, preferring to walk and collect my thoughts. I hadn't gotten far before I became aware of deep, booming music in the distance. I was drawn towards it and soon came across the impressive frontage of The Palace nightclub. A long queue of people stood outside, waiting to get in.

"Fudgey, quick, get in here," shouted Micky at the front of the queue.

It seemed natural to slip in next to him. Ignoring a few disgruntled remarks from behind, we shuffled towards the entrance. Once inside, we made our way to a bar upstairs which overlooked the dance floor below. It was heaving and swaying with people having a good time. I spotted Bull and Jim trying to dance. Someone tapped my shoulder and I turned round to see a seductive-looking Bev.

"Wow, you look gorgeous."

"Thank you," she smiled.

"I'll leave you to it," whispered Micky in my ear as he handed me a pint.

"Ok, mate, I'll catch up with you later," I said casually pulling out my pendant and letting it dangle over the front of my top.

Bev noticed it at once and reached out to examine it.

"What's this?"

With an air of mystic, I explained about my special talent for reading palms. Her face lit up and she excitedly began pleading with me to read hers. At first, I half-heartedly refused, taking delight in her increasing levels of desperation and persuasion. However, not wanting to let this attractive fish off the hook, I soon agreed to give her the reading she desired.

The Chill Out Lounge was a quieter part of the club and allowed revellers to talk to each other without shouting directly into the other person's ear. We sat down opposite each other. Bev held out her hand which I gently took in mine. It was soft and dainty and I began making a show of studying it. Sensing her eagerness for information I looked deep into her eyes.

"What the fok is going on here?" growled Dobbers towering over us.

Before I had a chance to explain, a brawl erupted. Fists flew and adrenaline surged. A couple of bouncers appeared and swiftly got us both into headlocks before unceremoniously dragging us off in different directions. I feared the worst as I was bundled through a fire exit into a corridor of bright lights and bare grey concrete.

Expecting a flurry of punches from my captor I was pushed through another door and out into a cold, dark alleyway where I began protesting my innocence.

"Fok off," was his response as he retreated inside.

Left in semi-darkness, I stared at the closed door and listened to the distant thudding of music coming from within. Relieved no more fists had flown I straighten my clothes and made my way out onto the street.

As I toyed with the idea of queuing up again, I heard someone shout my name.

In amongst a line of people waiting at a nearby taxi rank, I saw a familiar figure.

"AJ, what are you up to?"

"I've just come out of The Palace."

"Yeah, so have I."

"I didn't see you in there."

"I was only in there for a few minutes."

"*A few minutes*?"

"Yeah, there was a bit of a misunderstanding and I got thrown out by one of the bouncers."

She wiped a tear from her eye.

"What's the matter?"

"Oh, nothing, I'm just a bit upset about my gran."

It had been a long day and all I wanted to do was go home and get into bed. The image of AJ's boyfriend smooching in The Momtaz was still fresh in my mind and I couldn't help but feel sorry for her.

"Do you fancy walking home? I think we could both do with the fresh air," I said.

"Yeah, ok."

She peeled off from the queue and we began walking through the fluorescent-lit streets.

"Sorry about yesterday," AJ said.

"That's ok. I didn't realise you had a boyfriend."

"Yeah. Hugo. He's lovely, isn't he?"

"But the other night didn't we…?"

"The other night?" AJ looked at me and shook her head. "Can't you remember?"

"Not really, I think someone spiked my drink."

"Spiked your drink? It might have had something to do with all the tequila slammers you had. You only stopped because they ran out of lemons."

"But what happened back at your place?"

"*Nothing* happened back at my place. We were the last ones to leave the ball. You were trying to finish reading my palm, but you kept seeing double and couldn't work out which lines were which. I tried putting you in a taxi, but you couldn't remember where you lived. I said you could come back to mine and sleep on the floor in my room, as long as there was no funny business."

"Oh, and was there?"

"No, there was not," she said abruptly, "you went straight to sleep — although you did somehow manage to slip into my bed during the night."

"Sorry about that. Where's Hugo tonight?"

"He had to take a client out to dinner."

"Oh, right," I said picturing Hugo with his *client*, "and what does he do for a living?"

"He's a property developer — he doesn't like to talk about it, but he's trying to pull off a big deal at the moment. If he can make it happen, it will make him a millionaire."

"If he doesn't like talking about it, how do you know?"

"I overheard him on the phone the other day," she said with a guilty look on her face.

"How did you two meet?"

"We met a few months ago. He just turned up at the cottage and asked if we would be interested in selling it."

"And were you?"

"No way. My great grandad built that cottage and the family have lived in it ever since."

"And that's the first time you met him?"

"Yeah, I guess it was fate."

AJ continued to tell me how wonderful Hugo was as we ambled along the streets until we eventually arrived at her garden gate. As we crunched down the gravel path to her front door, I began to think about what sort of kebab I would get on the way home. After a few steps, she stopped and turned around. Her watery eyes twinkled in the moonlight.

"Would you stay with me tonight?"

"Eh?"

"It's just nobody's at home and I don't want to be alone at the moment."

I was desperate to go home, eat a kebab and go to sleep in my own bed, but her hangdog expression proved too much.

"Sure, as long as there's no funny business."

"Thank you," said AJ giving me a friendly hug.

"Have you got anything to eat I'm starving?"

"How about bacon and eggs?"

"Sounds great."

The kitchen was warm and cosy — heated by a wood-burning Aga that dominated one wall. AJ lifted one of the large round lids on top revealing a metal hot plate where she placed a heavily blackened frying pan and poured in a big glug of oil. Sitting down at a sturdy wooden table I surveyed the humbleness of the old rustic kitchen. An old clock hung above the back door. An impressive white porcelain farmhouse sink, flanked either side by great wooden worktops, sat in front of a quaint little window. I tried peering through it, but the darkness outside meant I could only stare at the reflection of myself. I thought how different the evening could have been if Dobbers hadn't appeared.

Erotic thoughts were broken by the sizzling noise coming from the frying pan. AJ gently placed rashers of bacon into the hot oil. Marvelling at her skills, I watched as she agitated the bacon in the pan with one hand and cracked eggs into it with the other.

"Who else lives here?"

"Well, it's just me and my dad now, but he's gone on a fishing trip with my uncle for a few days."

"You don't mind?"

"No, he's been very troubled recently. Hopefully, he'll come back in a better frame of mind."

AJ placed a plateful of bacon and eggs in front of me.

"Thanks, are you having any?"

"No, Hugo says I need to lose some weight."

Outraged, I began protesting, but was taken aback when she began defending him.

"He's right though, Fudge, look at me," she said holding her hands out.

"He should love you for who you are, not what he wants you to be."

AJ half-smiled then turned and began washing up the frying pan. I gazed at her reflection in the window. A mournful look crept onto her face and I agonised whether to tell her about Hugo. I could handle the release of an embarrassing picture, but she looked so fragile and vulnerable. I decided now was not the right time. She put the pan away and sat down opposite me as I took my last mouthful.

"That was lovely."

"Thank you. Where did you get that?" asked AJ noticing my necklace that still hung over my top.

I looked down and gently caressed the pendant with my fingertips.

"Oh, this? My grandma used to be a fortune-teller. She gave it to me just before she died," I lied.

"Wow. It must run in the family then."

"Fudge, would you be able to tell me about my future? It's just that I'm finding the past a bit too painful at the moment. I just want to know things will be ok."

"Sure," I said, eager to shine some rays of sunlight into her life. "Before I start though, there's one important question."

"What's that?"

"Have you got any booze?"

"How about some brandy?"

"That'll do."

AJ rolled her eyes and disappeared into the lounge, returning moments later with a bottle of brandy. She poured two generous measures into a couple of thick glass tumblers before adding some ice. I took a swig as AJ held out her hand across the table.

Although I hadn't read all of my palm reading book, I'd made sure to read the section on marriage, confident the topic would be of eager interest to the owner of whichever hand I was holding. I felt uncomfortable doing it, but I was willing to try anything to cheer her up.

Gently holding her hand, I felt reassured in the knowledge that whatever I said about her future she couldn't dispute it. Once again, I made a show of examining various lines. Her hand felt softer this time. She tried to stifle a small nervous laugh.

"AJ, you need to take this seriously," I said with a smile. "Trust me, I'm a professional."

Tilting her palm, one way, then the other, I let out a few groans of intrigue as I got into character.

"Leave it out, Fudge," AJ protested. "Don't give me all that flannel, just tell me what you can see."

I looked near the base of her little finger for a small horizontal line.

"I suppose you want to know when you're going to get married?"

She could hardly contain her excitement as she briskly nodded and shuffled to the edge of her seat.

"Can you see this line running horizontally under your little finger?"

"Yeah, what does it mean?"

I recognised it as the marriage line. The book had explained how to work out the person's approximate age by its position between the base of the finger and the heart line. I took a few more seconds to study it.

"What does it mean?" she repeated slightly annoyed.

"Well, that's your marriage line, and looking at the position of it I'd say you're going to get married within the next year."

"Oh, Fudge," she said excitedly, "that's great news — I knew Hugo was the one."

She got to her feet and began twirling around the kitchen.

With mixed emotions, I picked up my drink and jokingly made a toast to the *happy couple*, but inside I was being torn apart with every pirouette.

"I can't wait to tell Hugo," she proudly announced.

"You can't," I snapped.

She stopped dancing and looked at me with surprise.

"AJ, you mustn't try and force things — you need to let them happen naturally."

"Oh."

"You can't mention any of this to Hugo."

"Why?"

"Because of the butterfly effect."

"What's that?"

"It's where a tiny change can have a ripple effect that dramatically alters the original outcome."

"Oh, hark at Einstein."

Raising my eyebrows, I pretended to look annoyed.

"Ok, ok, I won't tell him."

AJ looked up at the clock.

"Come on, we'd better get some sleep, I've got to be up early for a seminar. I'll make you a bed on the floor in my room, but this time make sure you stay in it."

She grabbed some bedding and made a makeshift bed consisting of two thick duvets and two plump pillows on the floor next to hers.

"Thanks again for staying tonight, Fudge. I really appreciate it."

"It's not a problem," I replied slipping fully clothed in between the two duvets, "probably best if you don't mention it to Hugo though."

"Why? He wouldn't mind. Don't tell me it's because of the butterfly effect," AJ said as she turned off the light and got into her bed.

Nestling my head on the pillows, I stared into the darkness and was quickly taken back to The Momtaz. The image of Hugo and his fancy woman was still fresh in my mind as I agonised whether to tell AJ. The pure elation I'd witnessed in the kitchen made my decision even harder, but I took a deep, silent breath and began to speak very softly.

"AJ, there's something I want to tell you. Before I met you tonight, I did a shift in The Momtaz. Well, I say a shift it was more like an hour, but anyway, when I got there, I had to chop a load of chillies."

Somewhat embarrassed, I continued to explain how I'd ended up washing my private parts in a basin in the customers' toilets. Grateful AJ didn't laugh, I quickly continued.

"Well, anyway, that's not what I wanted to tell you. It's what I saw in the restaurant when I made my way to the toilets."

I took another deep breath.

"Hugo was in there — sat at a table — kissing a young lady. I'm so sorry AJ, but I just had to tell you."

I lay in silence, imagining all the emotions that must be racing around her head.

Through the darkness came a faint sound. Straining to hear what I thought was a whimper — I heard the same sound again. To my utter dismay, I realised it was the sound of AJ gently snoring.

"Fokkin goodie," I whispered.

Chapter Four

The next morning, I woke up relieved to still be in the makeshift bed on the floor. Next to me was a note from AJ.

Gone to the library to work on my assignment. Thanks for staying over. Might see you at The Academy later for student night.

P.S. Slam the front door shut when you leave.

The curtains gently swayed as a cool breeze came in from the open window. Sinking my head back into the warm, soothing pillow, I began to think about my dilemma. Taking some comfort from the fact I had lifted her mood, I decided it was best to let AJ continue on her new, joyful path, for as long as possible.

I convinced myself to say nothing about Hugo. If there was anything untoward going on she would have to find out for herself. Having decided on this course of action I drifted back to sleep.

Soon, I was dreaming about holding Bev's soft, dainty hand and looking deep into her seductive eyes. Running my finger nonchalantly across her heart line I explained I could see she was in a toxic relationship, but not to worry as she had already met her future husband who would take care of her — and their three beautiful children. She gave me a knowing smile which instantly turned into a frown as we were interrupted by a piercing ringing noise.

Gradually, I became aware of my head moving from side to side on the pillow. My desperate attempt to go back to sleep was short-lived. The sudden shrill of an electronic doorbell caused my eyes to spring open. I lay motionless staring at the ceiling. It rang again.

"Are you stupid or what, nobody's in," I whispered without any hint of irony.

Filled with a sense of dread, I got up and crept across the room towards a cumbersome dressing table that was in front of the window. Being careful not to knock over any of AJ's beauty products that littered the top, I leant over and tried to see who was at the front door. A large oval mirror at the back obscured my view. Craning my neck over the top, I peered out through a small gap in the curtains.

Hugo was standing in the garden holding a plastic bag. I stepped back and caught sight of my terrified reflection. A firework display of questions exploded inside my head.

My thought process was frantic. Has Hugo got a key? Can I jump out of the window? If I can't jump, where can I hide? What if I can't hide? What will I say if I'm cornered? Could I beat him in a fight? Why is there lipstick on my cheek?

I heard Hugo's posh voice.

"Come on, I told you nobody would be in."

Leaning forward I noticed a young lady loitering next to a small red sports car nearby.

"Come on, hurry up, we need to get this done quickly."

As she got nearer, I recognised her from The Momtaz and could tell from her demeanour that she was uncomfortable being there. Hugo held open the bag he was holding.

"Here, grab some of these."

They pulled out handfuls of what looked like asparagus. I leant further forward and saw them pushing them into the soil behind the colourful rose bushes that ran along the sides of the cottage.

"Are you sure this is going to work?"

"Oh yes. Just make sure you get them as close to the walls as you can."

Puzzled why he would be secretly planting asparagus around the cottage I carefully stood back from the window. Pondering Hugo's actions, I looked at the mirror and noticed a photo tucked into the frame. A little girl stood in the middle of two women who were holding her hands. Each had a beaming smile.

Leaning over the assortment of beauty products, I plucked it from the frame to take a closer look. On the back, someone had written, *Amy with her mum and grandma - 1975*. Knowing what the future held for the little girl, I felt a tinge of sadness. Turning the photo back round, I stared at the joy on AJ's face before placing it back where it belonged. As I tried to slip it into the frame, I accidentally knocked over a can of hairspray. To my horror, beauty products began falling in all directions. My unsuccessful attempts to halt the domino effect only made matters worse. The ordeal eventually concluded with a perfume bottle teetering over the edge before smashing on the floor. An intense wave of perfume rose up as I stared at the broken glass.

Adrenaline had already put me on high alert and when Hugo shouted up at the window, I felt another shot course through my veins.

"AJ, is that you? Darling, are you up there?"

Edging away from the dresser, I hoped Hugo didn't have a key. The doorbell rang again. Taken back to my hide and seek days I quickly scanned the room looking for somewhere big enough to conceal me. The wardrobe would have been ideal back in the day, but I was too big for it now. My only realistic option was under AJ's bed. The doorbell rang again as I wriggled underneath.

I lay there, expecting to hear the sound of his footsteps coming up the stairs. The bottom of the bedroom door became the focus of my attention as I waited anxiously for it to swing open.

I waited — my breathing became shallower with every passing moment. I thought I was going to pass out. The doorbell rang again. In the distance, I heard the faint sound of a police siren.

The bastard's called the police, I thought, probably told them there's a burglar in the house.

The louder the siren got the more distraught I became. Weighing up my options, I decided it would not look good if I was discovered hiding under the bed by police sniffer dogs. Reluctantly, I shuffled out of my hiding place and made my way downstairs as the siren grew louder. The doorbell rang again.

The only plausible excuse I could think of was I'd been in a deep sleep and had just woken up. I tried to convince myself it was a good thing the police were coming — at least, if Hugo did lunge at me, they could step in and arrest him.

With half-closed eyes, I opened the front door and gave a mock yawn. My eyes widened and I stood for a moment taking in my surroundings — nobody was there. The sports car had gone. A police car blared past along the road in front of me. Leaning back against the open door, I listened to the siren fade into the distance. My eyes aimlessly fixed on the coat rack in the hallway as I tried to figure out what was going on.

A few moments passed before I realised I was staring at a dark green trench coat — similar to the one I'd seen in the woods. I stepped forward. My heartbeat accelerated as I put my hand inside the pocket. The doorbell rang. Terrified, I jumped backwards and bounced off the front door causing it to slam shut behind me as I fell outside onto the gravel path. Dazed, I looked down at my clenched fist and slowly unravelled my fingers to reveal an old brass Zippo. A skull and crossbones were engraved on it, encircled by the words *Humpo – Born to Ride.*

The doorbell rang inside the cottage and I looked up at the button on the front door. Gingerly rising to my feet, I went over and studied it more closely. The doorbell button was stuck in.

Using my fingernail, I managed to prise the button back out and stop the intermittent ringing.

"What a plum," I muttered.

Keen to return the lighter to the coat pocket, I tried to open the front door, but it was locked. And after a few frantic attempts to open it, I begrudgingly put the Zippo in my pocket before turning my attention to the nearest flower bed.

Behind the rose bushes, small green stalks poked out from the ground. Walking around the cottage, I found more pieces plugged into the soil up against the ageing stonework. Pulling one up, I knew straight away it wasn't asparagus and thought they might be cuttings from a rose bush which he'd planted as a romantic gesture.

Gradually, I became aware of my surroundings at the back of the cottage. I was standing in a well-kept garden. A rickety wooden shed stood at the far end next to a thriving strawberry patch. Putting the small piece of vegetation into my pocket, I went over and helped myself to the biggest one I could find. Taking a bite, I looked out over a stone wall at the back of the garden and across an overgrown field that sprawled out in front of me. A few houses were dotted around the perimeter, and in the far distance, I could see the broccoli-shaped treetops of the woods beyond. Reminded of the macabre situation I found myself in I decided to head straight to the police station with my latest piece of information.

A gust of wind blew an empty black bin liner across the garden. I watched it being tossed around for a while before it landed at my feet and nestled around my legs. My thoughts turned to AJ — she'd lost her mum when she was little, she'd recently lost her gran, I was unsure whether her boyfriend was a lying cheat who was up to no good and now there was a chance her dad was a murderer.

*

It was lunchtime when I approached the police station and after a glance over my shoulders, I made my way in. On explaining to the officer behind the reception desk why I was there I was shepherded into the depths of the building and once again the door to *Interview Room 1* was opened before me.

"Take a seat," he said before leaving me alone with my thoughts. I sat down hoping things would soon return to normal. The heart-wrenching voice of the mother played over and over in my mind. It felt like she had been talking directly to me.

The door swung open and DI Cashun strode in.

"Ah, Mr Fudge, I understand you have some important information."

Showing him the lighter, I proceeded to tell him about the trench coat.

"I think AJ's dad is the man you're looking for."

DI Cashun sat back in his chair and stared at me.

"Well, that's a bit of luck, because when we questioned the staff in the Halloween Café, they couldn't remember anyone coming in that fitted your description — but they could remember Rambo and his wife coming in," he paused before adding, "stinking of booze."

"Are you saying I'm a liar? I'm trying to do the right thing — do you think I'm here just for the sake of it?"

The detective did little to appease my annoyance as he continued in the same dismissive manner.

"You do know, that after a thorough search of the woods and at a huge financial cost to this police force, nothing whatsoever has been found."

"Well, that's hardly my fault. I only told you what I saw."

"Quite," he replied, "and now you're telling me the person you saw in the woods might be the father of a girl you spent last night with. Who incidentally has a boyfriend you don't approve of and believe might be up to no good."

"But the trench coat does look very similar. And there was a Zippo in the pocket."

"Look, Mr Fudge, lots of people own trench coats and Zippo lighters. You need to see a photo of this man or better still meet him in person. If you're sure it's the man from the café, let me know and I'll send an officer to make some inquiries What's the address?"

"Err, I don't know, but I could take you there."

"I don't think so," he dismissed, "just find out if it's him or not and let me know."

As he led me back out through the corridors he noticed my necklace.

"What's that?" he asked casually.

I explained about the pendant and my reasoning behind it.

"So, you like making things up do you?"

"No, it's not like that."

"Mr Fudge, if there's one thing I can't stand, it's a bullshitter."

I trudged out of the police station feeling completely despondent. Reaching into my pocket, I felt the piece of vegetation and asked a passer-by where the nearest garden centre was.

*

After a few wrong turns, I finally arrived at my destination and looked for the oldest member of staff, assuming they'd have the most knowledge of all things horticultural.

Spotting a wiry old man attending to some pot plants I approached him with trepidation.

"Excuse me, Bert," I said, noting his name badge.

The old man stopped what he was doing and gave me his full attention.

"Yes, young man, how can I help you?"

I showed him the suspicious item.

"Would you be able to tell me what this is?"

Bert began to study it.

"Where did you get this?"

"What is it?"

"This, my boy, is Japanese Knotweed. Where did you get it?"

"Err, my gran came across it growing in the wild when she was out walking. She wanted to plant some in her garden."

Bert grabbed my arm.

"Do not plant this anywhere."

"Why?" I asked as alarm bells rang in my head. "What's Japanese Knotweed?"

"This is an invasive weed," he said looking at it as if it had mystical powers, "once it starts growing, the roots will easily burrow into hard surfaces like tarmac, concrete, brick walls. I've known of cases where whole houses have had to be knocked down because of this little bugger."

I tried to remain calm.

"Oh, that's no good. I'll tell her not to plant it. I don't suppose you've got something similar she can grow, but won't mean she'll have to knock her house down," I said nervously laughing.

"Well, I've got some lovely green bamboo shoots that are harmless and look similar."

*

Later that afternoon, I caught up with Bull in the bookies and gave him the rundown of recent events. He tried to show a small amount of interest in between studying the form, placing a bet, shouting expletives at the TV screen and throwing his screwed-up betting slip into the bin. Only after the conclusion of the last race of the day did this routine finally come to an end.

"Come on, Bull, it's student night at The Academy tonight. I need to meet AJ there and tell her what Hugo's up to."

"What's Hugo up to?"

"Have you been listening to a word I've been saying?"

"Yeah…well, not really."

"Come on," I said somewhat dejected, "let's go and get that five-gallon barrel of scrumpy to line our stomachs before we go out."

I could tell Bull was secretly relieved that there were no more races to gamble on, and after a short walk, we arrived at the off-licence. The barrels were ominously stockpiled in one corner of the shop. A small, elderly Asian man sat behind a counter. The top of his head was just visible above the till.

"Can we have a barrel of scrumpy please?" I asked.

He peered around the side of the till.

"Do you want a broom handle with that?"

"*A broom handle*?"

The shopkeeper nodded as if it was a perfectly natural accompaniment.

"Five pounds deposit, refunded when you bring it back," he replied, adding to the confusion.

"No, thank you, just the scrumpy," I scoffed handing over twenty pounds.

Putting my fingers through a small metal loop on top of one of the barrels I managed to raise it slightly off the ground. The weight caused me to lose my balance and I set the hefty barrel back down again. The shopkeeper smiled and waved a broom handle in the air.

"Are you sure you don't want this?"

"How is that going to help?"

The diminutive shopkeeper rose from his chair adding a negligible amount to his height and walked over. Using slight touches with his hands he positioned the pair of us on either side of the barrel then threaded the broom handle through the metal loop. Without the need for any further instructions, Bull and I grasped opposite ends of the handle and picked up the barrel.

"Well, that's a lot easier."

The shopkeeper held his hand out. "Five pounds please."

*

We walked back with the barrel gently swinging between us. Arriving home, we found Micky in the front room sprawled across the settee watching TV.

"Alright mate, fancy a bit of scrumpy before we go to The Academy tonight."

"Yeah, I'll just watch the end of this," he said nodding at the television.

"Are you sure you should be watching that? We haven't sorted the TV license out yet."

The day we moved in the landlord had advised us to get a license as soon as possible as he'd heard there was a TV detector van operating in the area. We assured him we would get one. We hadn't.

"It'll be alright. There's more chance of Elvis knocking on the door than the TV license man."

Out in the kitchen, we carefully lifted the barrel onto the table allowing the small plastic tap at the bottom to hang over the edge. Bull got a pint glass and a pack of cards and placed them next to it.

"Come on, Bull, let's have a taste."

As I placed the glass under the tap there was a loud knock at the front door.

"I don't believe it," said Bull, "that better be fokkin Elvis."

Quietly putting the glass back on the table, we slowly made our way to the front room. Standing on either side of the doorway, we peered in, being careful not to let the mystery caller see us through the net curtains. Micky was now lying face down on the carpet, inching his way towards the TV, as if he was on a Special Forces operation.

"What are you doing?" I whispered.

He looked around, held a finger to his lips then pointed at the window. There was a figure trying to peer in.

Using his elbows, he slowly continued his journey across the floor until he was in range to press the *off* button with the finger of an outstretched arm. The screen went black and the television fell silent.

The figure at the window loomed large as it cupped its hands around its eyes and pressed its face against the window straining to see through the net curtains. Micky froze with his arm still outstretched. The shadowy form moved from one side of the window to the other and looked in again. Agonising seconds passed before the silence was broken.

"Is that you, Micky? What are you doing on the floor?"

"It's Jim," he said getting to his feet.

He hurried to the front door and let him in.

"You nearly gave me a heart attack," said Micky with his hand on his chest, "we thought you were the TV licence man."

"Sorry, I forgot my house key," he smiled.

We welcomed him in and made our way to the kitchen where Bull proceeded to pour a small amount of murky orange liquid from the barrel. He held it up to the light.

"Look at the state of that," he said before taking a swig. His whole body contorted as he swallowed and through a screwed-up face managed to say, "fok me — it's lovely."

The rest of us took it in turns to taste it. Our faces and bodies distorted to varying degrees.

"It will take some getting used to, but after a few pints, I'm sure it will taste like nectar," I said after wrestling to control my gag reflex.

I picked up the pack of cards and we all took a seat around the table.

"Right, let's play the *Ace of Spades* game."

"How do you play that?" asked Micky.

"It's really simple. I deal the cards out and whoever gets the *Ace of Spades* has to down a pint."

Jim filled the glass to the brim and placed it in the centre of the table. It was the prize nobody wanted to win.

Four separate emotions revolved around the table as I began to deal. First, was an overwhelming sense of dread felt by the player whose turn it was to receive a card. It had been hard enough drinking a small mouthful, let alone a whole pint. This feeling was deliberately dragged out by me, pausing before turning over each card, except on my go when I turned the card over instantly.

We all knew there was no escape when the chosen card appeared. The rest of us would immediately, and noisily, demand every last drop was drunk before the game could resume.

If you managed to dodge the chosen card the second emotion felt was immense relief. You could relax for a moment and almost enjoy yourself as you watched the other players squirm.

With two cards left before your go, relief quickly turned to hope. And with only one card to go, hope turned to desperation. Knowing this was the last chance of a reprieve your eyes would bore into the top of the pack hoping to see the *Ace of Spades* turned over. If it wasn't, the next round of emotions would begin and dread would rise once more.

At the conclusion of the game, when the chosen card was dealt, the four emotions would be replaced at the table by two vastly differing ones. A crushing sense of foreboding by the loser and one, jointly experienced by the remaining players, of sheer elation.

"Fok," was all Bull could say as he stared at the *Ace of Spades* in front of him.

Overcome with a deep nauseous sensation he shut his eyes and allowed his head to loll back on his shoulders. A crescendo of noise rose around him as we began whooping, jeering and banging the table in a wild, almost tribal, celebration. Unbridled euphoria swept aside the various emotions that moments earlier had swirled around the table. After composing himself, he let his eyes slowly open, and with a fixed determination, looked directly at the murky fate that awaited him.

Placing the glass in front of him, I added a few extra rules.

"It's got to be drunk in one go and no spillages."

The noise level rose higher as he brought the glass up to his lips, paused for a moment, and then started to gulp it down. He looked in pain as he swallowed each mouthful. His eyes began to water as he fought to consume the foul liquid. The clamour turned to congratulations a few moments later when he triumphantly slammed the empty glass back down on the table and let out an almighty belch.

"Easy," he spluttered unconvincingly.

Without any delay, Jim refilled the glass and returned it to the centre of the table.

The first few rounds were quite even. Everyone drinking their fair share. It wasn't the finest vintage and a few of us struggled to down our penalty in one go. Any spillages were dealt with by me, Judge Fudge, who always ordered extra scrumpy to be consumed.

Bull was the first to run out of luck, losing three times on the trot. He struggled to see off the first two pints of his losing streak and was visibly deflated when the chosen card appeared in front of him for the third time in a row.

The ensuing uproar was the most vociferous yet as he protested and tried to introduce a new rule where two pints in succession was the most anyone should have to drink. He was shown no mercy and eventually accepted his fate.

Reluctantly, he picked up the glass. Battling every fibre in his body, he began to guzzle the pungent solution. His eyes watered as he took noticeably smaller and smaller gulps before finally placing the empty glass on the table. The smug look on his face was soon replaced with horror as he regurgitated a small amount from his stomach. Swallowing hard as a chorus of jeers erupted, he could sense his manliness being challenged. During a lull in his queasiness, he boasted how he'd only been sick once in his life, and that was when he was a baby. However, moments later, everyone leapt from their seats as he projectile vomited all over the table and the game was brought to an abrupt halt.

Micky helped Bull up the stairs to the bathroom and made him kneel in front of the toilet.

"Well, that's the first casualty of the night and we haven't even gone out yet," said Jim, "perhaps we better eat something to soak up the booze."

"Good luck with that," I replied, "there's sod all in here."

Jim began to rummage through the cupboards.

"'Old Mother Hubbard's kitchen has got more food in it than ours."

The sum total of his foraging resulted in him finding a small screwed-up bag covered in ice at the back of the freezer containing a handful of peas. And from the bin, two slices of bread with hints of light green mould.

"If I pluck the mouldy bits off the bread, we could have a pea sandwich."

After giving a look of disgust, I suggested we use the cover of darkness to do a bit of garden hopping'

"Sounds good to me."

Leaving Bull and Micky in the house, we went out in search of something to eat.

"We're bound to find some fruit or maybe even the odd vegetable patch."

Jim nodded sagely and we set off into the night. Outside, we vaulted straight over the fence and into our neighbour's garden.

It brought back memories of the nights I'd spent garden hopping when I was younger. The thrill of the unknown. Using only the light coming from the windows to guide me to the next fence, trying not to get detected. People going about their business, unaware of the intruder on the other side of the window.

"There's nothing to eat in here, let's try the next one," I said before scampering across the lawn and disappearing over the next fence.

Garden after garden offered nothing. The routine of vault, survey and scamper was occasionally interrupted by the need for extra vigilance when we had to dart across a dimly lit road. Our search almost ended when, instead of the usual wooden fence to leap over, we were confronted by a high stone wall. Not to be defeated, we clambered on top of a pile of logs that had been neatly stacked up against it, placed our hands on top of the wall and catapulted ourselves over. Landing with a thud on the other side we quickly scurried into the darkness. The light from the kitchen window crept just far enough up the garden to illuminate a bird table complete with three wire bird feeders full of redskin peanuts hanging from it.

"Jackpot," I said.

We waited for any sign of movement inside the house before slowly creeping forward and grabbing a feeder each. Soon, we were murmuring with delight as we greedily chomped on handfuls of peanuts.

Hugo appeared at the kitchen window causing me to spit out the half-eaten contents of my mouth. Unaware of our presence, I watched as he began pouring a cafetiere full of coffee into two cups.

The window was slightly ajar and I faintly heard him ask, "milk and sugar?"

Still reeling from the shock, I quickly positioned myself under the window while Jim retreated into the darkness with his nuts.

Slowly raising my head, I used a small pot plant that was on the window sill for cover. Looking between the leaves, I watched on as Hugo handed over a thick brown envelope to a smartly dressed man with thin glasses and greased back hair.

"Consider this a goodwill gesture."

The man opened the envelope and ran his thumb across a wedge of fifty-pound notes.

"There'll be a lot more where that came from once you get the planning permission sorted for that field."

"You need to buy the cottage first. I didn't think the owners wanted to sell."

"Don't worry about that. Soon they'll be desperate to get rid of it."

A loud commotion erupted behind me. Hugo and his associate looked towards the window as I instinctively ducked down. Looking around, I saw the bird table on the floor with Jim underneath trying to wrestle the third bird feeder free. Keeping my head down, I scuttled across the lawn.

"Quick, we need to get out of here," I said pushing the bird table to one side. Jim reached out but only succeeded in pulling my necklace off as I hauled him up. I watched helplessly as it twinkled to the ground and disappeared into the grass. A quick fruitless fumble was all I could afford before giving up the search and chasing after Jim as he sprinted towards the stone wall.

Panic, adrenaline and scrumpy combined to give us extra strength as we leapt into the air. With outstretched arms, we managed to get our fingertips on top of the wall and hurl ourselves back over. Landing clumsily on the pile of logs on the other side, they immediately gave way and spilled across the lawn. Desperate to put as much distance between ourselves and the bird table we continued to vault fence after fence until we eventually arrived back, breathless, in the kitchen.

"You prat," I said between breaths, "you pulled my necklace off."

"Sorry, mate," Jim gasped, producing a half-empty bird-feeder, "do you want a nut?"

We laughed as the tension lifted, but a loud knock on the front door startled us. Exchanging worried looks we were relieved when Micky came bounding into the kitchen.

"Come on, lads, the taxi's here. I've just checked on Bull and he's out for the count, so it's just us three."

We let out a huge sigh.

"What have you two been doing?" he asked noticing us breathing heavily and looking rather dishevelled.

"We'll tell you on the way," Jim said, oblivious to what I'd witnessed through the kitchen window.

We followed Micky out through the front door towards the waiting taxi. All three of us squeezed into the back and we sped off towards the nightclub. The proximity of the taxi driver stopped me from blurting out what I'd witnessed. Instead, I sat in silence, listening to Jim explain to Micky how he'd ended up under a bird table, then trying to convince him the scrumpy had somehow given us superhuman powers.

"Seriously, the wall must have been four metres high," he exaggerated.

*

Inside The Academy, we were confronted by a large, heaving dance floor. The layout of the club was impressive. It had been built in an old theatre. Lasers darted in every direction. A stage area at the back was devoted to the DJ who looked like he'd just landed in a spaceship made of mixing decks, laser lights and smoke machines. The whole ensemble was bookended by two massive speakers, which boomed out the latest dance tunes.

We stood for a while, taking in our surroundings, before turning around and admiring two large staircases which we had unknowingly walked between. They swept majestically up to the galleries above. In days gone by, people would have paid good money to sit up there and watch the performance below. But now, it acted as a place for people to go and get their breath back and have a chat away from the sweaty throng below. A few people walked down the stairs holding fresh pints. I made a drinking motion with my hand then pointed up the staircase.

Having got a round of drinks, we sat down at a table overlooking the dance floor and marvelled at the grandeur of the place. I looked out over the mass of people below, anxious to find AJ.

Jim and Micky were soon itching to have a boogie and made their way downstairs. I was happy to stay and continue scanning the crowd. Someone tapped me on the shoulder.

"Hello, you."

"Bev."

"Sorry about the other night, Dobbers is very protective over me."

"Is he here tonight?" I said looking over her shoulder.

"Yeah, he's down there dancing, but don't worry, I told him you were only reading my palm and he's all cool about it now."

"Thank goodness for that. How are you anyway?"

"Yeah, good thanks, apart from my car."

"What's the matter with your car?"

"Oh, apparently, one of the pistons needs replacing. I don't even know what a piston is."

Thinking she would be impressed, I tried to explain, but it soon became apparent from the glazed look on her face, she didn't have a clue what I was talking about. Undeterred, I proceeded to give her a demonstration. I held up my forearm with my fist clenched to represent a piston. With my other hand, I formed a loose circle using my thumb and fingers to represent a cylinder and wrapped them around my wrist. I then began to vigorously thrust my forearm up and down through the circle.

"When the piston gets to the top of the cylinder the spark plug ignites the fuel and sends the piston back down again."

Bev started laughing.

"That looks a bit rude."

Continuing to demonstrate the piston moving up and down, I began laughing — my actions did look rather obscene.

Unbeknown to me, on the dance floor below, Dobbers stood statue-still. Surrounded by a sea of gyrating revellers, he stared at us laughing in the galleries and came to the conclusion any over-protective boyfriend would — I was showing his girlfriend exactly what I wanted to do to her. Consumed by a volcanic rage, he charged up the staircase. I was completely off guard as he unleashed an almighty right hook to the side of my head. Darkness instantly descended.

Chapter Five

Days passed. I became vaguely aware of a pinging noise in the distance. Muffled voices occasionally floated softly around my head as I drifted along in a dream-like state. A fleeting strand of consciousness was regained the first time I picked out the words Mr Fudge. Subsequent mentions of my name resonated a little stronger each time.

A slight tingling sensation irritated the back of my hand. The pinging noise gradually got louder, and now and then I was aware of a faint voice beside me. It was softer than the others and I felt comforted every time I heard it.

In other moments, I found myself basking in warm sunshine beside a picturesque forest. But the day would soon turn to night. A hideous, double-headed monster would rise up, towering above me, causing me to contort unnoticed beneath the starched white bedsheets of my hospital bed.

Three days after being struck on the head my eyes flickered open. The brightness of the room only allowed me to squint, but I could see a needle going into the back of my left hand. Attached to it was a tube that led up to a bag of clear liquid hanging from what looked like a metal hat stand on wheels.

I heard a familiar ping and looked over at an expensive-looking machine by the side of my bed. More tubes and wires ran from it to various parts of my body.

On top of a table next to my bed were a few cards. Above them floated a helium balloon with *Get Well Soon* on it.

I wondered who might be unwell. My eyes drifted over towards the empty chair in the corner of the room before closing gently as I slipped back into unconsciousness. The next time I opened them a young lady was sitting there reading a newspaper. A furry black coat hung over the back of the chair. I tried to speak, but nothing came out.

Dreamily, I tried to figure out where I was and how I'd got there. Looking back at the young lady, I noticed the headline on the newspaper — *Student Put into Induced Coma after Assault in Nightclub.* Below was a picture of a young lady in a gorilla costume and a man wearing combat gear. They stood happily smiling underneath an archway of balloons. I looked lazily around the room before my gaze landed back on the picture. A faint whisper of a memory swirled gently around my head.

As I lay quietly gazing at the image, it gradually dawned on me, I was staring at a picture of myself. The surreal nature of the realisation was overwhelming and I closed my eyes. Moments later, I felt compelled to open them again and focus my attention on the picture of the young lady. Lethargically trying to recall who she was, I wondered why someone would want to assault her in a nightclub.

Pursing my lips, I tried to speak, but no sound came out. I tried to move and was alarmed when I remained motionless. Incapacitated, I stared at her, hoping to make eye contact. Engrossed by whatever she was reading, her face looked familiar and I felt encouraged that a distant memory may be returning. In my dreamlike state, my eyes flickered between the picture and the lady reading the paper until it slowly became apparent — it was the same person.

As she turned the page her eyes glanced over the top of the paper and she immediately began to smile.

"Oh, Fudge, you're awake," noticing the confused look on my face, she added, "it's me, AJ."

Again, I tried to speak, but nothing came out.

"Don't try and say anything, Fudge. The doctor said you need to take things slowly. Just blink if you can understand what I'm saying."

I blinked.

"Oh, hang on, how do I know you weren't just blinking anyway?"

She thought for a moment.

"I know, blink twice if you can understand what I'm saying."

I blinked twice. She was jubilant and quickly went to inform one of the nurses who came in and checked my heartbeat, blood pressure and the bag of fluid that hung from the stand. She wrote down her observations on a clipboard at the end of my bed, told me to take things slowly then left the room. AJ pulled her chair closer and sat down.

"Can you remember what happened? Blink once for no and twice for yes."

I blinked once.

She showed me the front page of the newspaper.

"That brute, Dobbers thought you were trying to chat his girlfriend up. He came at you from behind and punched you. The doctor said your brain was that swollen they were thinking about removing the top of your skull to relieve the pressure." She paused. "Ewww, imagine that. Fortunately, they managed to reduce the swelling by pumping you full of drugs. The doctor said you were lucky your skull wasn't fractured. Anyway, you'll be glad to know, Dobbers has been arrested and kicked out of college."

Staring at the picture, it struck me, I was the *student* who had been assaulted. AJ noticed me studying the picture.

"Sorry, Fudge, the papers were desperate for a picture and it's the only one anyone had. It's from The Freshers Ball."

She continued talking whilst my attention turned to my surroundings and for the first time it hit me — I was in hospital. Hearing the words 'bad news' I felt compelled to listen.

"It looks like we're going to have to sell the cottage and the field behind it. Hugo spotted an unusual type of weed growing in the flower beds. He got a friend of his, who's apparently an expert on these matters, to take a look. It's something called, Japanese Knotweed, and it's almost impossible to get rid of. This friend of his said the roots have already started to penetrate through the walls and begun to crack the brickwork. I can't believe it."

She paused to wipe a tear from her eye.

"He said it's gone past the point of no return. So, the cottage — my home — will have to be knocked down. Hugo said the place is worthless now, but bless him, he has offered to pay eighty percent what the market value was before the weeds started growing so we can buy another place."

A kaleidoscope of colours exploded in my head. I tried to speak but only managed a faint, incomprehensible murmur.

"What is it, Fudge? Are you ok?"

She leant in, placing her ear next to my mouth, hoping to decipher what I was attempting to say. The sanitised smell of the room was replaced by the sweet scent of perfume. Another memory flickered and once again I tried to speak. Constructing a sentence in my head, I was aware by the time the words left my lips, all form of recognition had been lost. The more I tried, the more frustrated I became, until suddenly, the machine by my bed began to make high-pitched noises. A short, rotund nurse with a shock of grey hair rushed through the door.

"He was trying to say something," AJ said as she backed away from the bed.

The nurse pressed some buttons on the machine and the normal pinging sound returned.

"Well, let's not rush things my dear. It's good that he has regained consciousness, but I think that's enough excitement for one day," she said, assuming something more amorous had been going on.

"I'm sorry, it's just that, I think he was trying to say something," AJ repeated.

The nurse picked up the clipboard and scribbled down her observations before returning it to the end of the bed. After a quick look at her fob watch, she informed AJ visiting time was nearly over then left the room.

"I suppose I'd better go," she said picking up the furry black coat from the back of the chair. As she put it on, she felt into her pocket.

"Oh, I nearly forgot," she said, pulling out a gold necklace with a pendant on it. Transfixed, I watched as she held it up. A small, golden hand, hypnotically swung from the end.

"Hugo gave me this as a present. I told him you had one exactly the same. What are the chances of that? You should have seen the look on his face when I told him."

The jewellery glistened in front of me as disturbing slithers of memory began to return.

"Jim told me you lost yours. I hope you don't mind, but I want you to have this one. It's not my thing anyway."

The nurse returned.

"Come on, time to go. Visiting hours are over."

Without acknowledging her, AJ placed the necklace neatly on the bedside cabinet, kissed the ends of her fingers and softly touched my head.

"See you soon."

Shutting my eyes, I drifted into an uneasy sleep.

*

The following day, a sinister dream, loosely resembling the story of *Jack and the Beanstalk*, was cut short when I was awoken by a presence in the room. A smartly dressed man, with a familiar face, was sitting in the chair swirling something shiny on the end of his forefinger. Catching sight of the gold hand-shaped pendant as it whizzed around, I immediately felt vulnerable. Shutting my eyes, I listened to the soft whirring sound as the jewellery cut through the air and began to recall further fragments of my recent past. The room fell silent and I lay for a while, willing the unwelcome visitor to leave.

The silence continued to the point where I was convinced the disagreeable guest had left, but as I prepared to open my eyes, I heard a loud exhalation.

Disappointed, I waited a few moments longer before opening my eyelids by the narrowest of margins. Through the mesh of my eyelashes, I watched the figure rise from the chair and closed them again.

The heels of his expensive leather shoes click-clacked across the hard hospital floor towards the bed. Sensing him tower over me, my imagination ran wild. I prayed he was there out of a genuine concern for my well-being.

"Oh, Fudge. Poor, defenceless Fudge. Once again, you seem to be in the right place, at the wrong time."

The upper-class accent did little to disguise the alarmingly evil manner with which the words were spoken.

"Skulking around in my back garden — who knows what you might have seen, or heard? But with so much at stake, I simply can't afford to take the risk. I'm sorry it had to come to this, old bean."

A torrent of unsavoury memories swept over me as I recognised Hugo's voice.

"AJ will be so upset, but hey-ho, I'm sure I can let her cry on my shoulder one final time. She told me you were some sort of fortune-teller, well I bet you didn't see this coming."

I opened my eyes. Hugo froze. The outstretched fingers of his hands stopped just short of my neck as the door behind him swung open.

"What the fok are you doing?" shouted Bull.

Hugo looked deep into my eyes before spinning around waving the necklace in the air.

"Just putting this back on," he said, forcing out a smile.

"Oh, I thought…"

"To be honest, I feel a bit uncomfortable about putting it on him anyway. I assume you're his friend, maybe it's better if you do it," he said tossing Bull the necklace.

He turned back to look at me.

"See you soon," he said with an eerie smile, then swivelled on his heels and click-clacked out of the room.

"AJ said you were awake. You can put that on yourself when you get better."

Bull put the necklace back on the bedside cabinet along with a folded-up newspaper which he was carrying.

"What have you been up to?" he laughed as he moved the chair nearer to the bed and sat down.

Bull was oblivious to the fear in my eyes as I tried to speak.

"Are you ok mate? Who was that bloke?"

"Bad man," was all I managed to croak.

"Batman? Fok me, have you been on the tequila worms again? Anyway, how are you feeling?"

Desperate to be understood, I tried to say the words more clearly.

"Bad man"

"Bad man? Awww mate, I'm not surprised after what you've been through. The doctor said the brain scan revealed no lasting damage and they are hopeful you'll make a full recovery. You just need to give it time"

The last thing I had was time.

"I tried to get a message to your mum and dad, but they've gone on holiday. Probably celebrating the fact that you've moved out," he chuckled.

"Anyway, I can't stay long, it's student night at Mad Joes tonight and I won't be able to visit you tomorrow as I'll be slipping into my Tina Turner outfit. The student union has organised a massive fancy dress pub crawl around town which kicks off at midday."

The door began to open causing a sudden spike on the heart monitor. A nurse walked in and looked straight at the machine.

"It's only me," said the familiar face as she started to run through her routine checks.

I hoped Bull would suggest the blink once for no, twice for yes, game. He could save my life if he asked the right questions. I imagined using just my eyes to communicate in what would have been the worst game of charades ever. But, not only were my hopes far-fetched, they were also short-lived, as the nurse looked at her fob watch and informed Bull that visiting time was over for the day. After returning the chair to its original position, he said his goodbyes and hastily left the room. The nurse followed shortly after.

It was clear, the only person who could help me now was myself. Fearful for my life, I began trying to move various parts of my body, desperate to regain some strength before Hugo's next visit.

The next few hours were spent willing various parts of my body to move, but little by little my resolve ebbed away. Not even the slightest movement was forthcoming. As each minute ticked by towards the start of the next day's visiting hours, I became increasingly resigned to the fact that Hugo may well be able to execute his evil plan.

Eventually, my efforts dwindled to nothing, and with mixed emotions, I found myself reminiscing about happier times spent with family and friends. But every time my spirits began to lift, they were invaded by thoughts of Hugo.

In the past, I'd always stood up to people with wicked intentions, but Hugo was in a different league. And standing up to him now was not currently possible. The unseen effort to move had taken its toll and I began to resign myself to my impending doom.

The thought of Hugo tricking AJ out of her family home, so he could benefit from his scheming plan, consumed me as I lay helpless on the bed.

My vision began to blur as tears accumulated in my eyes. Closing them shut, I screwed out the excess and felt a cold sensation as the clear liquid streamed down the side of my face.

When I opened them again, I looked over at the bedside cabinet and noticed the newspaper Bull had left behind in his haste to go clubbing. The headline read — *Desperate Mum in Heartfelt Plea.* There were two pictures underneath, one showed a sad lady at what appeared to be a press conference flanked by two women police officers and the other was the familiar face of the missing girl.

A chilling collection of memories flashed through my mind as my gaze flicked between the mother's inconsolable look and the picture of her innocent daughter. More tears rolled down my cheeks as I remembered the encounter in the woods.

Eager to seek justice for the little girl, I channelled the anger rising inside me, and with renewed determination, concentrated on moving my toes. An hour passed without the merest hint of a twitch.

Feeling disheartened, I decided to focus on my fingertips and within minutes deflation turned to elation when I witnessed the slightest movement in the tip of my index finger. In time, I gradually managed to wiggle all ten of them. The effort took its toll and every time despondency crept in I would summon extra strength by looking over at the two pictures.

The combination of saving my own life and avenging the taking of another gave me added motivation to carry on. It was deep into the night when, after the jubilation of raising both my arms in the air, I allowed myself to get a few precious hours of sleep.

*

At daybreak, I was woken by a nurse checking my observations. She was pleasantly surprised when I gave her a raspy, "good morning."

"Well, well, look at you making progress," she said as I began to use my arms to haul myself up the bed into the upright position.

"I still haven't been able to move my legs though."

"Don't worry, it will happen in time. You can't rush these things," she said as I struggled to sit up.

"Here, let me help you."

Once I was sitting up, she gave me an electronic pad.

"If you ever need help with anything just press the button with the picture of a nurse on and someone will come and see you straight away."

"Ok, thanks. Would it be possible to have some breakfast? I'm starving."

"Of course."

The nurse soon returned with a bowl of cereal.

"If you manage to eat your breakfast without any problems, I'll see about getting some of these tubes removed."

Initially, I struggled to hold the spoon, but after a few mishaps I managed to get the hang of using it, and by the time I took my last mouthful most of my dexterity had returned. When the nurse came back, she was pleased to see the empty bowl.

"Right, we can do away with this now," she said as she removed the thin oxygen tube that ran across my top lip, "and if you're not sick, I'll come back to remove these wires and the drip as well. You're making great progress, Mr Fudge, keep it up."

I held onto the control pad and waited.

As soon as visiting hours started the door swung open and in strolled Hugo carrying a black leather briefcase.

"Hello," I said sarcastically.

"Oh, you're up."

"Yeah, sorry to disappoint you — and before you think about trying any funny business, one press of this button and the nurse will come running," I said showing him the control pad.

"Funny business? I don't know what you mean," he smirked, "I just thought I'd pop in and see how you were."

"I'm doing great. The doctors think I'll be out soon."

"That is good news. AJ will need a shoulder to cry on," Hugo sneered. "Oh, and when you do get out, don't bother going round to the cottage."

"Why?"

"Because it won't be hers anymore — it will be mine. Well, it will be briefly. I'm going to sell it to a housing company, along with planning permission for the field at the back. Before long, it will be turned into a nice new housing estate. I'm meeting the solicitor there at four o'clock to get all the paperwork signed," he said shaking the briefcase.

"Soon, I'll be a millionaire. Oh, and don't worry, by the time you get out, I'll be long gone. There are two plane tickets in here for me and my real girlfriend to start our new life abroad."

"You bastard. After all AJ's been through."

"She'll get over it," he dismissed.

Instantly consumed with hatred for the man who stood before me, I found myself fantasising about the possible barbaric methods of torture AJ's dad would subject him to once his devious plan was exposed.

Hugo wished me an insincere farewell.

"You'll never get away with it," I shouted as he left.

Dejected, I tried to work out a way of getting a message to AJ. But without a phone number or an address, my hopes dwindled fast.

The nurse came back, congratulated me on my empty bowl then removed the wires and drip from the back of my hand.

"How soon do you think it will be before I can leave?"

"Well, that depends. You've got to remember you've suffered severe trauma to your head. Thankfully, your injuries weren't as bad as we first thought, but you still can't rush these things. If all goes well, I'd say you could be out of here within a week."

"A week," I spluttered, before composing myself, "do you think it would be possible for me to have a wheelchair? I want to try and make my own way to the toilet."

"Of course, but don't try and do too much too soon."

*

A short while later I was staring at a battered old wheelchair and began to recall the day spent helping AJ with her assignment. With renewed impetus, I threw back the bedsheet to reveal my unresponsive legs and set about manhandling them off the side of the bed.

Managing to get into a sitting position next to my bedside cabinet, I paused for a moment to readjust the flimsy backless gown I was wearing. Emily stared up at me from the newspaper, spurring me on. My necklace hung from the corner of a *Get Well* card. I put it back on before continuing to manoeuvre myself into the wheelchair.

A great deal of exertion followed before I eventually slumped into the chair. After taking a moment to get my breath back, I let the brakes off and edged towards the cabinet.

Inside, I found my wallet, the packet of Turkish cigarettes and Humpo's brass Zippo lighter. Placing them on my lap I wheeled myself out into the ward and made a beeline for the exit.

"Where do you think you're going?" asked the matron who was sitting behind the reception desk. "You're not allowed to leave the ward."

"Oh, I was just looking for the toilet."

"Over there — where it says toilet," she said, dismissively pointing at the other end of the corridor.

Giving a fleeting smile, I rolled back past her. On arriving outside the toilet, another palaver ensued, as I tried to open the door and get inside. Eventually managing to get through the doorway, I hoisted myself onto the toilet with the help of some strategically placed handrails and sat contemplating my next move.

With my only escape route blocked, I resigned myself to going back to my room. Feeling completely deflated, I wheeled myself back along the corridor. A loud, piercing alarm startled me. Matron rushed past, followed by a team of nurses. I watched as they all stormed into a room further down the corridor where a red light flashed above the doorway. Seizing the opportunity, I turned my chair around and sped towards the exit. But at the last moment, I was stopped by a nurse coming the other way.

"What are you doing? You're not allowed off this ward."

Thinking fast, I waved the packet of cigarettes at her.

"I'm desperate, this is the first chance I've had to have one since I came in."

At first, she refused, but I continued pleading as my eyes kept being drawn to the room the matron had disappeared into.

Sensing my desperation, she reluctantly agreed as long as a porter pushed me to the smoking area and brought me straight back once I'd finished.

*

"Thanks for doing this," I said over my shoulder to the tubby middle-aged man who had been tasked with the job.

A short journey in a lift and several corridors later I was wheeled towards a set of automatic sliding doors which parted as we approached. Outside, I filled my lungs with fresh air as warm sunshine beamed down on me.

"Here we are," said the porter as we arrived at a small shelter littered with discarded cigarette butts.

Figuring out what to do next, I put a cigarette in my mouth and clicked open the Zippo. A few small sparks appeared when I struck the flint wheel, but the wick failed to ignite.

"Oh no, it looks like I've run out of lighter fluid," I said, trying to sound disappointed. "Have you got one I could borrow?"

"No, I haven't."

There was a short silence.

"Sorry to be a pain, but could you please go and get me one."

Unable to hide his irritation, he stormed off in search of a lighter, uttering a few expletives as he went. As soon as he disappeared back through the sliding doors, I span around and began speeding off in the opposite direction, following signs for the main exit.

In my desperation to put as much distance between myself and the porter, I became aware that I was attracting unwanted attention from staff and visitors alike. The thin gown I was wearing flapped in the breeze, exposing various parts of my body.

It felt like I was trying to escape from a maximum-security prison and half expected a loud siren to start blaring, accompanied by the ominous sound of barking dogs.

To make my getaway less obvious I slowed down to a more sedate pace and before long I was experiencing the exhilarating feeling of freedom as I coasted out of the main gates. A bus, displaying the words *Town Centre* above the windscreen, was waiting at a nearby bus stop.

The driver was much more skilled at deploying the ramp than the previous one I had encountered. And soon, I was looking out of the window at a world I hadn't seen for a while, as the bus lazily made its way into town.

On arriving in the town centre, I descended slowly back down the ramp, and within minutes I was applying the brakes on the wheelchair as I pulled up outside The Palace nightclub. I allowed myself a few minutes to get my breath back, but the thought of Hugo made me release the brakes on the wheelchair sooner than I would have liked. Time was running out to thwart my nemesis.

Having a vague recollection of the previous walk I had made with AJ back to her cottage, I began to retrace my steps. Weaving through the bustling town centre, a few individuals caught my eye — Father Christmas, Elvis, Snow White. Recalling Bull mention something about a fancy dress pub crawl, I kept a hopeful eye out for a blonde wig and leopard-print dress.

It wasn't long before the physical exertion began to take its toll and I was forced to stop for a rest. Bathed in warm sunshine and feeling drowsy I was powerless to stop my eyes from shutting and within seconds was drifting into a deep sleep.

A short while later a group of female students dressed as sexy nurses walked past on their way into town. Waking briefly, with my eyes half open and my head lolling on my shoulders, I overheard their conversation.

"Awww, look at that lightweight, he's drunk already," said one.

"Look at the effort he's gone to with his outfit, he's even got one of those name tags on his wrist," another one pointed out.

"We can't leave him here. We'll have to look after him, at least until he sobers up. We are supposed to be nurses after all," laughed a third.

I fell asleep, unaware I was being pushed back towards the town centre, where they took it in turns to wheel me from pub to pub. The more the group drank the less concerned they were about my welfare, until I was eventually abandoned in the enclosed beer garden at the back of The Gander on The Green. Rousing from my sleep, I became acutely aware of the unsavoury nature of the conversation that seemed to be going on around me.

My eyes flickered open and I found myself surrounded by a blur of hefty bikers, clad in varying amounts of leather and denim. I thought I was back in hospital having another one of my dreams — Jez came into focus, sat directly in front of me.

"You've got some nerve boy," he growled, "coming back here."

Confused, I took a few moments trying to work out where I was and how I'd got there.

"Where am I?"

Jez shook his head as he scanned the faces of his cronies that were gathered around.

"Unbelievable," he said taking a look at his watch, "quarter to four in the afternoon and he's drunk already. Fokkin student lightweight."

I began explaining my predicament. Adding, the reason I looked like a hospital patient in a wheelchair was not an elaborate fancy dress outfit, but because I *was* a hospital patient in a wheelchair.

"Do you think I'm stupid?" Jez asked.

Tempted to say yes, I opted for showing him my wristband instead.

"Look."

Jez grabbed my hand and took a closer look. As he studied it his menacing look softened slightly and he let go. Again, I explained my dilemma to the sceptical audience.

"Let me get this straight. You're telling me you did a runner from the hospital because you're trying to get to your friend's place before four o'clock otherwise she's going to be tricked into selling her home by her unscrupulous boyfriend."

He glanced at his watch again. "Well, good luck with that, you've got ten minutes to get there."

Everyone around me began to laugh and I slumped back in the wheelchair. Helpless to stop my eyes from welling up, I felt the urge for a cigarette. Putting one in my mouth, I went to light it with the Zippo. Once again, it failed to light, causing another wave of laughter.

With as much dignity as I could muster, I put the cigarette back in the packet and placed it back on my lap, along with the lighter.

"Excuse me," I said letting my brakes off.

I began to manoeuvre myself past Jez, but he stuck out a large leather boot in front of one of the wheels, causing the chair to turn sharply and we ended up face to face.

"Where do you think you're going?"

Not caring what my fate was and with nothing left to give I looked him square in the eyes and said, "oh, fok off."

The surprised look on his face was accompanied by sniggers and a few mouthfuls of lager being spat out by his companions. Instantly regretting my outburst, I began to try and pacify the situation.

"AJ recently lost her mum and now she's going to lose her home. I was the only person who could have done anything about it and now…"

Whilst deciding my fate, Jez's attention shifted to the Zippo. He reached out and seized it from my lap.

"Where did you get this?"

"AJ's dad, I…erm…borrowed it."

"AJ?"

"What?"

"This girl, you said she's called AJ."

"Yes, it's short for Amy Jones," I said expecting to be belittled at any moment.

"Hasn't Humpo got a daughter called Amy?" he asked, showing the now curious faces the engraving on the lighter.

"Yeah," said one of the bikers, "and he did mention something about having to sell his place."

Jez looked at his watch.

"Right comrades, we've got just over five minutes to get there."

The back gates to the beer garden were quickly flung open to reveal a row of gleaming motorbikes parked on the road outside.

"Right, you're coming with me," Jez said as if he was expecting me to leap from the wheelchair.

All I could do was sit there with my arms outstretched. After rolling his eyes he wrapped his burly arms around me, scooped me up out of the chair and slung me over his shoulder. The backless gown made no attempt to hide my naked buttocks as I was paraded on the short journey to his gleaming Harley Davidson before being unceremoniously dumped on the back.

"Boney, fold that wheelchair up and bring it with you," he said to a tall, balding biker with a sidecar attached to his bike.

After slapping a matt black helmet on my head, he kick-started his motorbike. A deep rumble reverberated off nearby buildings as a chorus of beefy machines fired into life.

Leaning forward, I told Jez it would be helpful if someone could pick up a man called Bert from the garden centre.

"Sleebob," he bellowed as he dismounted. I watched as he went over to the grey-haired rider of a large trike and told him to make a detour.

Returning moments later, we were soon accelerating away. The sheer power almost caused me to fall off the back, but I managed to lunge forward and coil my arms tightly around his waist. The intimate nature of the embrace and the musty odour that emanated from his jacket made for an uncomfortable ride.

As we winged our way at high speed towards the outskirts of town, I kept catching sorry glimpses reflecting from passing shop windows. My thin gown flapped furiously behind me like a low-budget superhero's cape.

On any other occasion, the experience would have been exhilarating, but all I could think about was getting to AJs before pen was put to paper.

*

Jez eased back on the throttle as the cottage came into view, but my relief soon turned to panic. A small red sports car and a top-of-the-range BMW were already parked outside.

The front of the bike dipped down as it skidded to a halt between the two cars. Jez kicked the stand out, leapt off, and then hurried down the garden path. From my position perched helplessly on the back of the motorbike, I could only watch as he began banging and shouting at the front door as the rest of the bikers swarmed around him.

A bemused Humpo appeared in the doorway, Jez pushed past him and they both disappeared inside the cottage, followed by the rest of the gang.

Boney appeared next to me with the wheelchair and after manhandling me into it left to join the others. Managing to singlehandedly negotiate my way through the garden gate, I soon ground to an abrupt halt on the gravel path. Desperate to get inside the cottage, all I could do was sit there and listen to the commotion that was coming from within.

After a while, AJ appeared shaking her head.

"Fudge, what are you doing out of hospital? What's all this nonsense you've been saying? It's those drugs you've been on."

The bikers streamed back out and congregated in the garden. Humpo, Weggy, Jez, Hugo and a smartly dressed man emerged from the property and began interrogating me. Hugo kept interrupting as I tried to expose his dastardly plan.

"What a load of rubbish. Look at the state of him, his medication is clearly playing tricks on his mind."

There was no denying my bedraggled appearance as Hugo continued to convince everyone of his innocence. I desperately tried to counteract the plausible explanations that Hugo effortlessly fired back to the point where I began to question my own far-fetched account of recent events.

"Look, guys, we need to get this poor, deluded soul back to the hospital where he belongs. He needs medical attention," said Hugo.

Feeling physically and mentally exhausted I was inclined to agree. A brief moment of double vision was followed by complete darkness as I flopped backwards into the chair.

Chapter Six

When my eyes eventually flickered open, I was relieved, if somewhat confused, to be back in my hospital bed. Looking across the room, I was pleased to see AJ sitting in the chair reading a magazine.

"Oi," I rasped.

"Fudge," she shrieked, quickly stuffing the magazine into a colourful fabric handbag on the floor beside her, "how are you feeling?"

"Oh, AJ, I've had the worst nightmare imaginable. I'm so glad you're here, I need to tell you something really important. I just hope I'm not too late."

I went into great detail telling her about the events that led up to the moment I confronted Hugo outside her cottage.

"And then, I just blacked out, before I could convince anyone."

AJ smiled.

"Oh, Fudge, it wasn't a nightmare, it actually happened."

"But what about your cottage, please tell me you didn't sell it? You all thought I was deluded."

"Well, you're right, we did all think you were deluded and I'm not surprised, what with the amount of drugs they've been giving you in here. What were you thinking, turning up to the cottage like that? Anyway, once the ambulance arrived to bring you back here, we went back inside to sign the paperwork."

"Oh no."

"The cottage had only been signed over to me a few months ago, when I turned eighteen, and there I was in floods of tears, selling it to Hugo."

A giddy sensation rose up and swirled around my head.

"AJ, the Knotweed wasn't real."

She put her hand in the air to silence me.

"Let me finish — I was just about to put pen to paper when Sleebob burst through the door, followed by a man called Bert, from the garden centre."

The very mention of the old man's name lit a glimmer of hope inside me. This soon exploded into a glorious starburst as AJ explained how Bert took one look at the so-called Japanese Knotweed and burst out laughing.

"He then went on to give us a long and in-depth description of what it actually looks like and the perils it can pose if you do ever discover it growing in your garden. He said what we were looking at was the harmless bamboo shoots that he sold you the other day. We found the actual Japanese Knotweed in a black rubble sack in the shed."

"Thank goodness for that. What did Hugo do?"

She took a moment to compose herself.

"He said he could prove he wasn't lying and went to his car to get the results of his friend's survey."

AJ paused to wipe a newly formed tear from her eye.

"And what happened when he came back with it?"

"Well, he didn't — he jumped in his car and wheel span off. I haven't seen or heard from him since."

"What a scumbag."

AJ pursed her lips and nodded.

"And then the police showed up."

"To arrest Hugo?"

"No, they were asking my dad a load of questions about the missing girl, and then they started searching the place. My dad was fuming. He said someone must have told them he had something to do with it."

The warm glow of contentment I was beginning to feel was pierced by the icy hand of dread as my thoughts turned to Humpo and the missing girl.

"As soon as you're well enough he wants to take you out for a thank you drink."

The expression on my face took AJ by surprise.

"What's wrong? You look horrified," she laughed, "it's ok, he doesn't bite, he just wants to show his appreciation for what you've done and take you out for a drink. You should feel privileged, I've only ever known him to go out with his biker friends."

A fumbled acceptance of the offer was received without any suspicion of trepidation before I quickly changed the topic and asked her how she was feeling.

Tears began to roll as she tried to bluff her way through an upbeat response, but it was obvious she had been deeply hurt.

"Men, they're all bastards," I joked.

AJ looked up and broke into a welcome smile.

"How come you didn't see this in my palm," she said waving her hand in the air, "some fortune-teller you are."

Trying to look offended I gave my pendant a gentle rub.

"Anyway, don't worry about how I'm feeling. How are you feeling?"

Instinctively I tried to wiggle my toes and we were both delighted to see the blanket ripple at the end of the bed.

"A lot better," I smiled.

"Look, I better be going, I want to go and lay some flowers on my grans grave and tell her all about what's happened, but I'll come back and see you a bit later, ok?"

"Of course, I'll look forward to it"

She playfully ruffled my hair and went to leave the room, but stopped in the doorway.

"I forgot to ask, what were you doing with my dad's Zippo lighter?"

My mind went into overdrive as I scrambled for a plausible explanation.

"I've got to be honest," I lied, "I haven't got a clue."

"Hmmm, well it's a good job you did have it. If Jez hadn't seen it, things would have turned out a lot worse."

AJ's parting words kept haunting me. Her dad would know the only possible explanation for me having his lighter was I rifled through his trench coat and pinched it.

An elderly lady brought a temporary pause to my worries when she entered the room carrying a tray with my dinner on. With one hand she skilfully pivotcd the bedside table over my lap and with the other gracefully placed down a plate of stew and dumplings and a bowl of apple pie and custard.

After an exchange of pleasantries, I eagerly picked up my cutlery, but just as the first forkful approached my lips a doctor entered the room and I reluctantly placed it back on my plate.

"Glad to see you've got your appetite back, Mr Fudge. How are you feeling?"

"Ok, I suppose, I managed to move my toes earlier, but I have got a slight pain in my head and feel a bit drained."

"Yeah, I did hear about your bid for freedom yesterday. I don't suppose that's done you any favours," he said looking intently into my eyes whilst shining a small torch into them.

"Well, you seem to be making good progress," he continued as he picked up the clipboard at the end of the bed and studied it.

"Thankfully, the swelling in your brain has reduced significantly. It was touch and go at one point whether we needed to operate, but fortunately, the extent of your injuries weren't as bad as we first thought. As soon as we can get you up on your feet, we'll be able to think about letting you go home. Anyway, I'll let you eat your food before it gets cold."

"Would it be possible to have a walking frame?"

"Of course, as long as you don't try and do another runner."

After an over-the-top assurance, the doctor agreed and left the room leaving me to devour my meal. With each mouthful, I could feel my energy levels gradually return and vowed to set about getting on my feet as soon as I'd finished the last bite of apple pie and custard.

*

Wiping my lips with a paper napkin, I looked over at the newly arrived piece of walking equipment that had been left inconveniently on the other side of the room. I tossed the screwed-up napkin onto the tray and marvelled at the simplicity of the contraption — a dull grey aluminium frame with wheels on the front two legs and rubber feet on the back legs.

Once I'd moved the table out of the way, I threw back the blanket to expose my bare feet. A smile broke out as I watched my toes wave back. Soon, I'd managed to gently sway my feet from side to side. Within an hour, my legs began to respond and I lay back with mixed emotions.

The elderly lady returned to collect the empty plates.

"Good to see you've got your appetite back."

"Yeah, it was lovely, thanks."

"Getting your energy back for another escape?"

"No, no," I said, "but I do need to get out of here as soon as I can."

I asked her to move the walking frame to the side of the bed, which she duly obliged.

"Have they found that missing girl yet?"

"No, not yet. Her mother was on television again last night, making another appeal. It's heartbreaking to imagine what the poor dear must be going through. I just hope they find the girl soon," she paused before adding, "one way or another."

The last four words struck me like a lightning bolt. AJ would be destroyed to find out the truth about her dad, but I couldn't allow sentimentality to get in the way of justice. Enough time had been wasted and the harrowing thought of what might have happened to Emily and the torture that her parents must be going through galvanised my determination to get on my feet as quickly as possible.

Left alone in the room, I proceeded to shift my legs off the bed and place my feet on the floor. Leaning forward, I grasped the top of the walking frame with both hands and hauled myself up into a standing position. Supporting most of my body weight with my arms it wasn't long before they began shaking and I collapsed, disappointed, back onto the bed.

"Mr Fudge," said a voice of authority.

Assuming it was one of the doctors I looked up and was surprised to see DI Cashun standing in the doorway.

"What are you doing here?"

"I need your help. Do you mind if I sit down?"

The detective sat down without waiting for me to reply and went on to explain they were still searching for Emily.

"I'm afraid all lines of inquiry have drawn a blank. We've managed to track down this Humpo fella, but he has an alibi. On the evening Emily went missing he said he was at home all night with his daughter, but to be perfectly honest, Mr Fudge, I don't believe him one bit — he's hiding something."

"I know he is," I replied annoyed.

"Look, we've searched the property and found nothing," continued the detective sensing my irritation.

"How can I help? I've told you everything I know."

"I heard about your little escapade yesterday. I'd imagine Humpo must feel he owes you a huge debt of gratitude."

"I suppose. AJ did say he wants to take me out for a drink as soon as I'm well enough."

"Excellent. We'd better get you out of here as soon as possible so you can take him up on his offer. Once he's had a few drinks his guard will be down and hopefully, he'll let something slip. We'll sort you out with a recording device."

"*A recording device?*"

"Yeah, it's nothing to worry about," he said flippantly, as I pictured an enraged Humpo discovering the device and instantly subjecting me to a horrific ending.

"I'm sorry to have to ask you to do this, Mr Fudge, but you're the only hope we've got and I want to nail this bastard. We need to get the ball rolling as soon as possible."

The detective stood up.

"Call me as soon as you've been discharged and I'll send a car to pick you up. There are a few things we'll need to run through before your big night out."

I didn't appreciate him making light of the situation and shifted uncomfortably in my bed as he handed me a small card with his number on.

"Just in case you lost my last one."

Bidding me farewell he headed for the door but stopped short when it swung open and found himself face to face with AJ. Both were surprised by the presence of the other. The detective gave the smallest of acknowledgements then skirted around her as she in turn stepped to the side to allow his exit.

AJ watched the door close before turning around.

"What was he doing here?"

"Oh, he just wanted to ask me a few questions about…you know…what happened at the nightclub," I said pleased with my on-the-spot cover story.

"Blimey, he gets about. That was the same man who came round asking questions about the missing girl."

"Oh, wow, what are the chances of that?"

"He said he was making house to house inquiries of all the properties in the area. The thing is, I spoke to some of my neighbours afterwards and none of them had had a visit. It just seems a bit strange, don't you think?"

I could feel a warm flush develop on my face.

"Perhaps they weren't in when they came knocking."

"Maybe."

Feeling increasingly anxious, I was relieved when AJ noticed the walking frame.

"Are you able to walk now?" she said excitedly, instantly changing the mood in the room.

"Well, I stood up for a few seconds earlier. I just want to get out of here now."

"That's the spirit. Come on, let's go for a walk."

"A walk?" I spluttered. "Where have you got in mind?"

"Only to the door and back, come on, up you get."

Taking a firm grip of the walker, I heaved myself upright and with a little help from AJ, managed to shuffle towards the door.

"Well done," she said, giving me a small ripple of applause.

Inching the walker around, I made the short journey back to my bed. It was only a few steps, but I felt a great sense of achievement.

"Come on, Fudge, and again."

The next hour saw the walker being discarded in exchange for AJ's outstretched hands and with each minor achievement, a wave of adrenaline washed over me, spurring me on further.

The whole exercise was brought to an abrupt halt when AJ stumbled back onto the bed, inadvertently pulling me on top of her.

The door swung open and an elderly nurse stood aghast holding a pair of crutches.

"What the hell's going on in here? This is a hospital, not a knocking shop," she said, placing the walking aids at the end of the bed.

AJ unceremoniously rolled me to one side as we began protesting our innocence.

"Mr Fudge, please control yourself. You need to save these sorts of shenanigans for the privacy of your own home."

Further denials of guilt were met with very short shrift.

"Look, I've come to tell you your vital signs are back to normal and as soon as you can walk, even if you need to use those crutches," she said nodding towards the end of the bed, "the doctor said he would be happy to discharge you. Then you can satisfy your desires in a more appropriate setting."

Denying us a final opportunity to convince her of the misunderstanding, she strode out of the room.

Instead, we sat looking at one another desperately trying not to laugh. Fully aware that the irate nurse could overhear and burst back into the room to deliver a more explosive dressing down.

After taking a moment to compose ourselves, AJ rose to her feet and fetched the crutches.

"Come on, you heard what she said. Let's see how you get on with these."

I put my arms through the grey plastic hoops at the top of the bleak accessories and gripped the handles. Gingerly, I got to my feet. At first, it was a struggle to coordinate my arms, legs and crutches as I walked in a gangly fashion around the room.

After several short trips around the perimeter of my bed, I gradually began to walk in a more synchronised manner.

"Come on, let's go for a walk out here," said AJ holding the door open.

Grateful for a change of scenery, I willingly obliged and headed out into the corridor beyond.

A few treks up and down the passageway were accompanied by words of encouragement from nurses and patients alike.

"Well, well, somebody's keen to get home for a bit of rumpy-pumpy," said the nurse from earlier.

"It's not like…"

"Ok, ok, I'll have a word with the doctor," she interrupted before hurrying off.

Giggling, we headed back to the room where I flopped exhausted on my bed.

"Right, Fudge, I'm going to have to go now. Do you want me to get my dad to pick you up when you get discharged?"

"Err, no, that's ok. I've already got someone lined up to come and get me."

"Ok, but don't forget, he still wants to take you out for a drink. When do you think you'll be up for it?"

"As soon as I can get out of here. Maybe tomorrow night, if they'll let me out that is."

"*Tomorrow night*? Don't you think that's a bit too soon?"

"No, it will be fine, I'm gasping for a pint," I fibbed.

AJ departed shaking her head and I laid back down letting my lungs slowly deflate.

*

The following morning a doctor entered the room.

"Mr Fudge, the nurse informs me you're eager to be discharged."

"Yeah," I said, nodding hopefully.

"Ok, I'll see what I can do."

He left the room and I looked across to my bedside table at the small business card left behind by DI Cashun.

My internal monologue circled, darted and flipped between two extremes. I convinced myself I had no other choice but to go undercover and try to unearth Humpo's hidden secrets.

Emily's family needed answers, justice, closure, a mixture of all three. Whatever it was, I felt a deep sense of responsibility.

But within a heartbeat, I'd changed my mind. Why should I put my life on the line for someone I don't even know? Surely, in time, the case would be resolved, even without my intervention. I convinced myself to say and do nothing.

Every time I decided on the latter course of action, I instantly became lightheaded as I imagined DI Cashun listening to my pathetic excuses. My heart felt like it was trying to escape from my chest. It pounded against my ribcage as I pictured myself feebly trying to defend my cowardly decision.

*

A little over an hour later, I used my crutches to walk tentatively past DI Cashun as he held the door open to *Interview Room 1*.

"Thanks for sending the car. I've been thinking…"

"Yes, I bet you have," he said butting in, "you've been thinking about another way of doing this. Another way that doesn't involve you using a recording device. Another way that doesn't involve you going out for a drink with Humpo. Another way of avoiding Humpo altogether."

"Yes," I said enthusiastically, nearly falling to the floor. The detective pulled out a chair.

"Well, you can forget that. As I said before, you are our only hope."

My legs gave way and I collapsed backwards into it.

"Mr Fudge, you must try to remain calm. Humpo wants to take you out for a drink. All we're asking you to do is to take a small recording device with you."

After leaning my crutches where the table met the wall, I vigorously rubbed my face with my hands as if trying to wash away the fear.

"What if he suspects something and frisks me?"

The detective pulled out a packet of cigarettes from the breast pocket of his faded white shirt.

"Do you smoke?"

"Not really," I said pulling one from the opened packet.

He produced a brass Zippo lighter from his trouser pocket similar to Humpo's, but without the engraving. Instead, the word Zippo was embossed in silver lettering on the front. Holding it at arm's length, he flicked open the top with his thumb and struck the flint wheel causing a flame to rise from the wick. Lighting the end of my cigarette, I took a prolonged drag, hoping to reduce my soaring anxiety. But it only served to make me nauseous and light-headed.

Snapping the lighter shut he placed it on top of the cigarette packet in the middle of the table. Then, after folding his arms, leant smugly back in his chair.

With growing annoyance, I repeated myself.

"What if he suspects something and frisks me?"

DI Cashun didn't reply but instead let a beamy smile slowly develop on his face.

"What's so funny?"

Still smiling, he leant forward, picked up the lighter and began twirling it with his fingers.

"Do you know what this is?"

"It's a cigarette lighter," I said with as much indignation as I could muster.

"Yes," he said slowly, "but it's also a discreet recording device."

Staggered by the revelation, I watched as DI Cashun demonstrated how it worked.

"The 'Z' of Zippo is a secret button. If you press it, you trigger the device to start recording. To stop recording, simply press the 'o' at the end"

Taking the lighter I ran my finger over the 'Z'.

"Press it to record."

Gently shaking my head, I continued to marvel at the innocent-looking lighter.

"See, Mr Fudge, if you didn't suspect anything, Humpo won't either."

Dated spy films had led me to believe I'd be wearing a bulky device, gaffer taped to the small of my back. Attached to this, I assumed, would be a length of wire and a small microphone which I would also have to secrete about my person. The small, innocuous gadget, I now twiddled between my fingers, went some way to elevate the angst I felt, but not enough to escape the detective's watchful eye.

"Mr Fudge, I can see you're a little apprehensive, so let's keep this simple. You're going out for a few drinks — just go with the flow — be yourself. Maybe even try and enjoy yourself, but at some point in the evening, you will need to subtly drop into the conversation a comment about the missing girl. Everyone knows about it, so it won't seem unusual to casually mention it."

Nodding solemnly, I passed the lighter back to DI Cashun.

"There's eight hours recording time, so press the button just before you meet up. Then, at the earliest opportunity, light a cigarette and casually put the lighter and packet down in front of you," he said mimicking the actions as he spoke.

After placing both back on the table he sat back with his arms outstretched as if he'd just performed a magic trick.

"Easy."

Initial feelings of terror marginally downgraded into the realms of dread.

"I still wish I didn't have to do it though."

"I know, Mr Fudge, but just think of this poor little girl and her distraught family," he said, shrewdly pulling on my heartstrings, "you're their only hope of solving this case."

"What about Emily's dad, I thought he was a gangster, can't he do something?"

"He's a gangster, not a detective. And believe me, if he ever finds out who's responsible, I'm certain more people will go missing."

"Ok, ok, I'll do it."

"Good lad. You'll be fine," he said pushing the lighter and cigarettes across the table.

Putting them in my pocket, I reached for the crutches and rose to my feet.

"How are you getting on with those things?"

"Alright, I don't think I'll need them for too much longer."

"That's good. Do you want a lift home?"

"No, thanks, I could do with stretching my legs."

We walked to the rear of the building where he held open the exit door. The feeling in my legs had returned to such an extent that I felt a bit of a fraud as I made my way outside using the crutches.

"Oh, and one more thing."

I turned expecting a final piece of advice.

"Don't fokkin lose it."

I assumed he meant the lighter, but as I made my way home it occurred to me, he may have been referring to my state of mind.

Returning home to an empty house, the only thing that greeted me was a mountain of washing-up in the kitchen. The old flimsy worktop bowed slightly beneath the weight. Convinced it would snap in half if one more item was placed on top, I crept past.

The day had taken its toll and with the help of the banister I made the ascent upstairs. It was nice to return to my bedroom, even with the numerous takeaway containers that now littered the floor. I climbed into bed and drifted off to sleep.

Chapter Seven

A few hours later the bedroom light came on and Bull staggered in clutching a kebab. Reluctant to let go of the greasy pitta bread, he initially tried to get undressed one-handed. Hopping and banging around the room, he finally admitted defeat and placed it down on his bedside table. Sitting on his bed, he removed the remaining items of clothing before looking across the room and staring blankly at me for a few moments.

"Fudgey, you're back!"

Slurring his words, he began to tell me about a new nightclub called Glasshoppers, but gave up when a bout of hiccups took hold. I watched him struggle with his convulsions as he tried to remove his contact lenses before placing them in a glass of water next to his kebab. I fell back to sleep.

It was lunchtime when I woke up. Across the room, Bull was sprawled out on top of his bed, naked, apart from a Wolverhampton Wanders FC bobble hat that he was now inexplicably wearing. His hairy chest, along with a few morsels of onion, cabbage and doner meat, rose gently up and down. I smiled. It was good to be back.

"Bull."

His eyelids flickered open and he turned his head towards me.

"Fok me, when did you get back?"

"Blimey, you must have been steaming. Can't you remember? I was here when you came in last night. You were telling me about the new nightclub, Glasshoppers, but gave up when you got the hiccups. Then you put your contact lenses in that glass of water."

We both looked at his bedside table. Next to a half-eaten kebab was an empty glass. Bull reached out and picked it up.

"Oh, shit," he said gazing into it.

"Don't tell me you've drunk them."

"I've drunk them."

As I started to laugh a searing pain in my head gave me instant karma.

"It's not funny mate, they cost me fifty pounds. I can't see properly without them. I can't afford to get another pair," Bull said despondently.

Sensing the gloom in his voice, I apologised.

"There's only one thing you can do."

"What's that?"

"You're not going to like it."

"What is it? Tell me."

"The next time you need a shite you'll have to do it on a plate and have a look for them."

"Err, I am not doing that," Bull said adamantly.

"It's the only thing you can do if you want your lenses back. You've got until the next time you need a log to decide," I said with a grin.

"Goodie."

"Anyway, you'll never guess what DI Cashun wants me to do."

"What?"

Sitting up in bed, I told him about my secret mission.

"Are you mad?"

"Don't tell anyone what I'm up to. Apart from the police, you're the only other person who knows about it."

"I won't mate, I promise. Just be careful."

"I will," I said as my stomach began to rumble, "do you want the rest of your kebab?"

Bull noticed the remnants on his chest.

"Ah breakfast," he said daintily plucking the residue out from his hairs and eating it.

"I meant, do you want the rest of the kebab that's on your table? I'm starving."

Bull picked it up.

"Here you go," he said stretching out his arm and handing it to me, "careful though, it's got hot chilli sauce on."

"Thanks, mate — I think I can handle a bit of chilli sauce. What do you think I am? A man or a mouse?"

I took a bite and instantly spat it out.

"Flipping heck, Bull," I spluttered, "what sort of chilli sauce is on that?"

"I asked for the hottest sauce they had. I'm not sure what it was, but there was a skull and crossbones on the bottle."

Putting on my boxer shorts, I gingerly went to get a drink to cool my mouth. After a successful descent of the stairs, I arrived in the kitchen hoping to find a clean glass. Following a pointless search of the cupboards, I stood in front of the washing-up mountain, agonising over which glass was the cleanest. The worst ones had mouldy green residue in the bottom, but I managed to find a reasonably clean one in amongst the pile and gently pulled it out as if I was defusing a bomb.

To get to the tap I had to remove a pan full of brown slime which had been wedged between the contents of the gunky overcrowded sink and the underside of the tap. Prising it free, I carefully balanced it on top of the festering stack on the worktop before returning to clean the glass and fill it with cold water. As I did so I became aware of a quiet creaking sound that quickly developed into an almighty clatter as the worktop gave way and spewed out a mixture of pots, pans, shards of glass and broken crockery at my feet.

Careful not to stand on any shards, I inched backwards. Bull thundered downstairs shouting, "Fudge, are you ok? What's going on?"

Moments later, he appeared in the doorway holding his bobble hat over his genitals.

"Fok me, what have you done?"

"Have we got a dustpan and brush?" I asked.

"Leave it, mate, I'll sort it out later. At least there'll be a bit less washing-up to do now."

Heading into the lounge, we found Micky snoring loudly on the settee, without a stitch on, apart from his socks. The rest of his clothes were arranged in a neat pile on the floor next to him.

"Bloody hell, he could sleep through the apocalypse," I said.

"Yeah, he was spangled last night. We each did a bottle of vodka before we went out. Anyway, you lightweight, man or mouse you said. I better get you some cheese."

"Good luck with that. The only thing left in the cupboards is a tin of mackerel — and that was already there when we moved in."

Taking a swig of water, I tried to quell the burning in my mouth.

"I tell you what Bull, you're going to be in trouble when that kebab comes out the other end. It wouldn't surprise me if your ringpiece went down for a drink."

Bull felt a movement in his bowels.

"I'm not being funny, but I think it's about to make an appearance."

"Well, you need to quickly decide if you want your contact lenses back. Put it this way, would you flush fifty pounds down the toilet? Because that's what you're about to do."

Bull went back to the kitchen hoping to find a plate that survived the mini avalanche. Careful to avoid any broken fragments, he tiptoed through the debris. Finding one with a crusty dollop of mash potato still on it he headed upstairs and locked himself in the toilet.

Back in bed, I began to contemplate my night out with Humpo when I heard a blood-curdling scream. Throwing back the duvet, I hurried towards the door as fast as my recuperating legs would allow. Out on the landing, I came across Bull, crawling out of the toilet on his hands and knees. Behind him was the plate with a big steaming turd on it.

"It's a boy!!" he joked through a mask of tears.

"Did you find your lenses?"

"I haven't looked yet — my ring is stinging so badly."

"Oh, come on, Bull, are you a man or a mouse?"

"I think I'm going to pass out."

"What do you want me to do — get you some cheese?"

"No!! But you could get me some ice cubes."

After hobbling back downstairs, I opened the freezer to reveal an empty ice cube tray. Managing to scrape out a tiny bit of frost with my fingers, I returned upstairs.

"That's all there is."

I showed Bull the speckles of frost on my fingertips.

"That'll have to do. Rub it on my ring."

"Fok off," I said, slowly accentuating every syllable.

"Please, you've got to do something."

"Like what?"

"I don't know — blow on it."

Caught up in a whirlwind of irrationality, I reasoned this was a marginally better alternative. Reluctantly getting to my hands and knees, I began to gently blow on his ringpiece.

"What the fok is going on?" said a deep, booming voice.

Slowly raising my head over the top of Bull's anus, I looked at Humpo's horrified face on the staircase.

He'd stopped halfway up and stood gripping the banister, unsure where to look.

"It's not what it looks like. I can explain everything," I said, cowering behind Bull's buttocks.

"The hospital said you'd been discharged. I only came round to see when you wanted to go for a thank you drink. A naked man answered the front door and now I catch you cavorting about like you're in some sort of gay brothel. Well, you can forget that drink now you fokkin nonce."

Getting to my feet, I pleaded with the back of Humpo's head as it disappeared down the stairs.

"Who the fok was that?" asked Bull still wincing with pain.

"Humpo. AJ's dad."

"Hitman Humpo," said Bull edging backwards into the bathroom.

"What are you doing?"

"My sphincter is on fire. I'm gunna try doing a handstand under a cold shower and see if that helps."

Shaking my head, I made my way back into the bedroom to get dressed, then lay down on my bed. A wave of embarrassment washed over me as I pictured myself explaining to DI Cashun why the night out with Humpo had been cancelled.

*

A short while later, a fully clothed, pain-free Bull lay on his bed examining the lighter I had just tossed him.

"Fok me, it looks just like a real one."

"Yeah, it's not much use to me now though. I just feel really bad that I've let everyone down."

A fully clothed Micky opened the door.

"Alright, Fudge, it's good to have you back. AJ is on the phone."

"Goodie," I said looking at Bull.

"Mate, just explain exactly what happened. You've got nothing to hide, well almost nothing," he said lobbing the lighter back to me.

Downstairs, I tentatively picked up the receiver of the house phone and whispered into it.

"Hello."

"Fudge, is that you?"

"Yeah."

"What on earth is going on?"

Before I could formulate a response, AJ continued.

"My dad has just told me he walked in on you stark naked, rimming some bloke."

I'd never heard the word 'rimming' before, but after picturing the scene from her dad's point of view, I had a rough idea of what it meant. Eager to explain the misunderstanding, I did myself no favours with my opening gambit.

"I wasn't stark naked — I had my boxer shorts on."

Realising the implication of what I'd said, I launched into a desperate ramble.

The plausibility of my explanation was dubious at best. At first, it was met with a great deal of scepticism. But, after initially believing her father, my pleas of innocence eventually persuaded her otherwise.

"AJ, you've got to believe me."

Silence — then a muffled sound, like someone sobbing. My heart sank.

"Fudge, you really are something else," she said, trying to stifle a fit of giggles.

For the first time since Humpo had appeared on the staircase, a smile spread across my face.

"Oh, AJ, your dad must think I'm a right pervert."

"Well, yes. I've never seen him so angry. He's just been pacing around the kitchen, calling you all the names under the sun. In fact, if you take out all the swear words, he's only actually said *he*, *if*, *to* and *pineapple*."

"*Pineapple*? Why?"

"You don't want to know."

"Is he there with you now?"

"No, he's out in the field, shooting rabbits with his shotgun, trying to calm down."

Right on cue, I heard a dull bang in the background.

"Goodie."

145

"He doesn't know I'm ringing you, but I just couldn't believe what I was hearing."

"AJ, there's been a complete misunderstanding. Do you think you can have a word with him?"

"What? And explain how you ended up scantily clad on all fours, softly blowing into Bull's anus."

"Well, yes."

We both started laughing at the ridiculousness of the situation and after a few moments of cathartic amusement, AJ agreed to speak to her dad.

"I'm not promising anything. He really is in a stinker of a mood. I'll call you when I've spoken to him."

After thanking her profusely, I placed the receiver back down, hoping she would be able to convince her dad of the facts. I popped my head around the lounge door where Micky was spread-eagled on the settee, watching daytime TV.

"If the phone goes again, can you answer it for me, please?"

Micky nodded before looking up.

"Who was that bloke earlier?"

"AJ's dad."

"What's up with him? I only let him in because he said he wanted to see you — the next thing I know, he's storming out saying he'd never seen such debauchery. I'm not even sure what that means."

"Don't worry about it."

*

On my return to the bedroom, Bull was desperate to know the outcome of the phone call.

"I think she believes me, but whether her dad will is another matter. She's going to have a word with him."

Back on my bed, I was grateful for the distraction that Bull provided as he told me about all the nights out I'd missed whilst I'd been in hospital 'with my feet up'.

It was a welcome relief to listen to the idle gossip, until Micky, once again, poked his head around the door.

"That birds on the phone again."

Downstairs, I nervously picked up the receiver.

"Hi, AJ."

"Fudge, I've spoken to my dad."

My anxiety rose exponentially as I waited for her to continue.

"It took me a while, but I think I've convinced him there's been a monumental misunderstanding."

"You can say that again," I said sitting down on the bottom stair.

"He wants to know if you still want to go out tonight."

"Tonight?"

"Yes, don't worry if you'd rather not. I'm sure he'll understand."

There was a silence as I considered my response.

"He did say he'd pay for your drinks all night."

"I'd love to go out tonight, but tell him to be gentle with me. I'm still a bit doddery."

"Great, he said he'll pick you up about six o'clock. Have fun."

For the first time since DI Cashun suggested the idea, a small part of me looked forward to going out. I reasoned it was probably because I didn't want to risk further infuriation, rather than a desire to spend the evening in his company. Or maybe I was just desperate to go out for a drink.

The clock was ticking now. With only a few hours to get ready and clean the house I headed straight for the lounge.

"Micky, can you please do me a massive favour and tidy up the mess in the kitchen."

"Are you joking? Have you seen it in there?"

"Mate, please. AJ's old man is coming back to take me out for a drink and I need to get ready."

"Are you sure? The way he stormed out earlier I'm surprised he ever wants to see you again."

"Well, he does, so would you please tidy it up before he comes back? I don't want to antagonise him with that shit in there," I said pointing towards the kitchen. "I'll ask Bull to help you. I have been in hospital you know."

"Alright, alright," he said peeling himself off the settee, "what did your last slave die of?"

"Not tidying up the kitchen," I said with a wink.

*

It was just before six o'clock when I ambled into the kitchen wearing a pair of jeans and a garish yellow and orange Hawaiian shirt.

"What the fok have you two been doing?"

The kitchen table was piled high with the dirty crockery and kitchenware that had recently cascaded to the floor. Jagged edges of broken glass and ceramics poked out from the top of the bin by the back door. Micky stood in front of the sink looking like he was panning for gold as he swirled a frying pan under the cold tap trying to clean the grease off with his fingers.

"What the fok are you wearing?" asked Bull, who hovered next to him holding a tea towel.

"What?" I asked mildly offended. "Look, he's going to be here in a minute."

"Mate, we haven't stopped. We've only just finished clearing the floor," said Micky.

"Fok it, we'll have to do it later."

Grabbing armfuls of dirty washing-up from the table I frantically began shoving them haphazardly into the empty cupboards. Bull and Micky stared at me for a few seconds before joining in.

Soon all evidence of squalor was safely hidden away. As the last cupboard door shut the back door opened.

"Hello, guys. Nice to see you all with your clothes on."

Humpo stood in the doorway. The only evidence he'd made any effort to dress up was the thick red and blue collar of a lumberjack shirt that poked out from underneath his grubby denim jacket. However, the first thing I noticed was his clumpy black biker boots. Instinctively, I put my hand in my pocket and felt for the lighter.

"I did knock on the front door, but there was no answer."

"Oh, we were just, erm, doing a bit of spring cleaning. Sorry about the misunderstanding earlier."

"Don't apologise, Fudgey lad, these things happen. Are you ready to go?"

"Yeah, I just need my crutches. I'm still feeling a bit wobbly."

Chapter Eight

A beefy Harley-Davidson, with its smooth contours, was parked on the road outside. A couple of battered, open-faced helmets dangled from the chopper-style handlebars. My eyes were drawn to the two contrasting leather seats. The first one, which would soon have Humpo's derrière smothered over it was more like a saddle, but it was the passenger seat that impressed me. Raised above the back wheel, it looked almost regal, like a narrow leather throne. I viewed the tall backrest more as a safety feature rather than providing extra comfort.

Humpo put his helmet on before slapping the other on my head. It soon became clear that it was at least a couple of sizes too small as it sat perched on top. Not to be deterred, he proceeded to hammer it down with his fist as I struggled to stay upright, thankful for the support I was receiving from my crutches. Every thump caused my brain to reverberate in my head until eventually the helmet made it past my ears and Humpo decided that was as good as it was going to get.

With my grey matter still swirling, he set about tightening the straps, quickly giving up when it became apparent they were simply never going to meet under my chin and left them dangling by my cheeks.

"Oh well, just make sure it doesn't fall off," he said with a final slap on top of the helmet.

Swinging a leg over the seat, I hopped on holding my crutches. Humpo took his seat with much more grace before thundering the machine into life. An earth trembling twist of the throttle caused a few nosey neighbours to appear in their windows.

Holding both crutches under one arm, I tentatively wrapped the other around Humpo's generous waistline. Bull, Micky and Jim appeared from behind the net curtain in the front window, silently laughing and pointing as we sped off. We raced through the streets and I wondered where we were heading. Nothing too fancy, I gathered, considering the attire Humpo was wearing.

I took a few deep breaths of the air that streamed past my face hoping to curb my rising anxiety. It was beginning to work until in the distance I spotted a row of motorbikes parked outside The Gander on The Green. It hadn't occurred to me to enquire where I was being taken, but seconds later it became apparent as we pulled up alongside the rest of the machines.

Desperate for a drink to calm my nerves, I dismounted, prised off my helmet and followed Humpo inside. The smell of stale alcohol oozed from the dull, tacky carpet whilst a large, wispy cloud of cigarette smoke hung just below the nicotine-stained ceiling. In between the two resided a congregation of leather and denim wearing regulars.

As we walked through the pub a few shouts of 'Humpo' rang out and I was acutely aware of the looks I was getting from some of the unsavoury clientele. There was a heaving line of burly bikers at the bar. Various cloth patches with biking insignia were sewn onto the backs of their jackets —

The Piston Broke Club, *Bad to the Bone*, and an uncomfortable number of demonic-looking skulls. Jez was in amongst them and gave me a slight nod before turning back around.

Feeling uncomfortable in the macho environment, I scanned the room, hopeful for the soft features of any females. The one or two that I could see looked scarier than the men, with their bodies covered in tattoos and piercings.

Everything about the place unnerved me. My choice of brightly coloured shirt made me stick out like a beacon in the gloom of leather and denim. Humpo overheard a few sneers and came to an abrupt halt.

"Oi," he shouted glaring at the perpetrators, "he's with me."

Everyone stopped what they were doing. Even the jukebox, which was pumping out heavy metal, seemed to go quiet. I leant heavily on my crutches; aware I was the focus of attention.

After a few agonising seconds, Humpo broke the silence and casually turned to me.

"What do you want to drink?"

"A pint of cider, please," I said, hoping it was manly enough. Humpo nodded his approval and pointed to an empty table near a large window, through which I could see the row of bikes beyond.

"Take a seat over there and I'll bring it over."

I felt like Moses parting the Red Sea as rugged men moved aside to let me through. Those that were seated shuffled their chairs out of the way. Smiling politely, I hobbled through the newly created passageway. Nerves, embarrassment and fear caused me to overemphasise the use of my crutches. I added to the charade by giving a little wince of pain with every step.

One of the previously hostile-looking bikers stood by the table and pulled out a chair.

"Here you go, mate."

"Thank you," I said sitting down with a small sense of guilt.

Once seated, I placed my crutches on the grimy carpet under the window and tentatively scanned my surroundings. Apart from the odd glance, most people seemed to have adopted their previous positions. Through the crowd, I spotted Humpo snaking his way towards me. Reaching into my pocket I pulled out the cigarettes and lighter and placed them next to a large glass ashtray on the table in front of me.

Humpo arrived with two pints of murky orange liquid.

"Get your laughing gear around that."

Taking the closest one I held it up to the window wondering if there had been a mistake with my order.

"You can't beat a pint of good old rough cider."

Humpo picked up his glass and gulped a few greedy mouthfuls. I took a sip.

My face instantly screwed up as the acidic fluid hit my taste buds.

"Fok me."

"Good init?" Humpo replied, oblivious to my repulsion.

Desperate for something to take the taste away I reached for my cigarettes and pulled two of them halfway out of the packet.

"Do you want a fag?"

"Cheers," said Humpo taking one and helping himself to the lighter.

Bringing the packet up to my mouth, I pinched my lips around the other cigarette and slowly slid it out as I nervously watched Humpo examine the lighter.

"That reminds me," he said pulling out his own Zippo from his pocket, "what were you doing with this one?"

"Erm, I don't know. I must have picked it up by mistake."

Humpo looked at me suspiciously

"They are very similar," I added.

A grunt and a puff of smoke later he returned his lighter to his pocket and placed the other back on the table.

After a short uncomfortable silence, I lit my cigarette, secretly clicked the 'Z' of Zippo, and placed the lighter nonchalantly down in the centre of the table. Humpo took off his jacket and hung it on the back of his chair. Trying to act cool, I tilted my head back and added a steady stream of smoke to the velvety cloud above. When I looked back down, I noticed the marks on his arms.

"They're nasty scratches you've got there."

Humpo held up his powerful forearms twisting them one way then the other. The scratches weren't as angry now, but they were still prominent.

"How did you get them?"

Humpo looked dubiously at me.

"Gardening."

"*Gardening?*"

"Yeah."

Desperate to break the uneasy eye contact, I reached for my drink and swallowed a small mouthful.

"Well, Fudgey lad, I'm not sure how I can ever thank you for what you did."

"Oh, don't mention it."

"*Don't mention it?*" Humpo said almost enraged. "If it hadn't been for you, I'd have sold the cottage to that little weasel. I can't believe the lengths he went to. He must have been planning it for months. Ever since we refused to sell it. He only started going out with AJ to worm his way into our family. Did you know that?"

I nodded.

"That place has been our family home for generations."

"Have you heard from him since?" I asked meekly.

Humpo took a big gulp of cider.

"Don't worry. We won't be hearing from him again," he said with a wink.

"You haven't, erm..." Unable to complete my sentence, I drew my finger across my throat.

Humpo didn't answer. Instead, he drained the rest of his glass, wiped the back of his hand across his lips and rose to his feet.

"Come on, Fudgey lad, drink up. I'll get us another."

He stood over me, clutching his empty glass. I reached for my drink, wishing I'd asked for a fruit juice. Feeling like I'd just been dealt the *Ace of Spades*, I picked up the pungent beverage and began to guzzle it. A few drops escaped from the corners of my mouth and trickled down my cheeks as I desperately fought against my gag reflex. My body's instinct was to resist the consumption of the vile liquid, until eventually and somewhat triumphantly, I held my empty glass in the air for Humpo to refill.

"Good lad," he said, oblivious to my discomfort, "I'll be back in a minute."

As soon as he was out of earshot, I released an almighty belch. Repulsed by the putrid taste in my mouth, I took a long drag on my cigarette. Instantly regretting it, as the tobacco smoke compounded the dizzying effects I was already feeling from the alcohol.

Panic set in. Initially thinking I had all evening to glean some incriminating evidence, I could see my window of opportunity closing rapidly. Two, possibly, three more pints, and I knew I wouldn't be capable of rational thinking.

"Here you go, my boy."

Another two pints of gloom were plonked on the table. A small amount spilt from one and I instinctively reached for it, thinking one less sip might give me a few extra minutes of sobriety.

Possessing a modicum of Dutch courage, I pressed for further information about Hugo.

"I don't want to waste my breath on that low life," Humpo spat back clearly enraged.

I took a big swig of my drink.

"I'm sure I've seen you somewhere before," said Humpo unexpectedly.

Recalling our paths crossing in The Halloween Café, I began to protest.

"I've only just moved here. I must have one of those faces."

Humpo's eyes narrowed slightly.

"I can't quite put my finger on it. Your hair looks different. Have you done something to it?"

"Yeah, I'm always going to my stylist to get a new hair doo."

The beginnings of a smile crept onto Humpo's face.

"My daughter has taken quite a shine to you."

"Well, she's only human," I joked.

Humpo didn't laugh. His attention was drawn to the gold-plated pendant that had made an appearance from beneath my shirt.

"AJ said you were some sort of fortune-teller."

"Well, not quite — I read palms," I said shifting awkwardly in my seat, hoping he wasn't about to thrust his open hand across the table.

He thrust his open hand across the table.

"Go on then, read that."

"No, I couldn't. Not in here — there's not enough light," I said, hopeful of a reprieve.

"It's ok," he said shuffling his chair next to the window, "we can do it here."

Humpo was adamant he wanted his palm read and once again held his hand out as if he was expecting me to perform a magic trick. Terrified of causing offence, I tentatively took hold of it. The experience couldn't have been starker in contrast to the one I imagined when I first picked up *The Beginner's Guide to Palm Reading*. So far, my *mystical powers* had brought nothing but trouble.

I stared at the rugged paw in front of me.

Feeling slightly woozy, I made a final half-hearted plea.

"Are you sure about this?"

"Yes. I want to see if you're as good as AJ says you are," he said jabbing his upturned hand towards me. "I want you to tell me things that nobody else could possibly know."

Sensing an opportunity opening up before me, I began to examine the deep furrows that crisscrossed his hand.

Rolling the unfurled palm back and forth under the light from the window my gaze was drawn to the pale pink scratch marks further up his arm. I tried to stay focused but was helpless to stop the strong emotions rising from the pit of my stomach.

"Well, what can you see?" asked Humpo sharply.

Annoyed at his impatience, I looked him straight in the eye.

"I can see a death."

Humpo shot back a steely stare.

"Well, of course you can, my mum died, you know that."

Ignoring the comment, I examined his heart line closely.

"There's something else. I can see a burial."

"Like I told you, my mum passed away."

"I know, but this burial," I said pointing at a random line on his hand, "it's in the woods."

Looking at him quizzically, I saw a hint of fear in his eyes.

A loud bang on the window made us both jump. Bull, Jim and Micky were on the other side laughing, pointing and posturing effeminately.

"Cooeee," Jim squeaked through the glass.

Looking down at the palm I was tenderly holding, I realised how the scene may appear.

Humpo snatched his hand back.

"Cheeky bastards," he growled getting to his feet.

The three of them looked terrified and ran off as Humpo's large, angry frame, filled the window. Trying to diffuse the situation, I motioned towards his chair.

"Shall we continue?"

Humpo was noticeably flustered.

"Erm, I just need to go to the toilet."

I watched as he made his way across the pub before disappearing into the gents. Aware of the suspicious looks I was still getting, I sought comfort with a big glug of rough. Expecting to grimace as I swallowed, I was surprised at how quickly I'd become accustomed to the taste. Taking another swig, I looked down at the lighter, aware I needed more than a worried look to get DI Cashun's juices flowing.

Hopes of resuming the reading were dashed when Humpo returned. Silently pulling his chair back from the window, he returned it to its original position.

"I've got to be honest with you, Fudgey lad."

Humpo looked anxious. I glimpsed at the lighter.

"I think I'm going to need a lot of therapy."

"Why?" I asked tentatively.

Humpo leant forward, putting his elbows on the table and his hands over his face.

"It's ok, you can tell me."

I waited, hoping for a revelation.

"What is it?"

Humpo opened his hands, like a pair of doors, to reveal a troubled expression.

"I can't get that bloody image out of my head."

Fuelled by cider, I probed further. Daring to believe I was on the verge of a confession. Once again, I looked down at the lighter hoping his voice would be audible above the background noise.

"What 'bloody image'?" I asked impatiently.

Humpo put his hands flat on the table.

"The bloody image of you, stark naked, on all fours, softly blowing your friend's arsehole."

A few people in the surrounding area sprayed out mouthfuls of booze. It was obvious they had been secretly listening in on our conversation. Humpo began laughing and I reluctantly joined in.

"Seriously, it's going to take a lot of sessions before I can unsee *that*," he chuckled.

I consoled myself by downing the rest of my drink.

"Same again?" he asked.

Another two pints were soon on the table.

Humpo enquired about the incident in the nightclub, offering to 'sort out' the brute who put me in hospital. My instinct was to respectfully decline until I remembered the lighter.

"What do you mean by 'sort out'?"

Humpo's demeanour changed as he looked around to check nobody was listening.

"Look, Fudgey lad, what you did to stop our cottage falling into the hands of that scum bag was nothing short of a miracle. And no amount of drinks will ever be enough to repay you. I just feel I need to do more."

"I don't want you to kill him if that's what you mean."

"No, no. I wouldn't do that," he blustered, before leaning forward and whispering, "keep your voice down. You don't know who might be listening."

I looked around sheepishly.

"I think I'm being followed by the police," he said.

"What makes you say that?"

"You know that girl that's gone missing?"

"Yeah," I said as my heart accelerated.

"Well, the other day they came to the cottage — sniffing around — asking questions."

My heartbeat reached top gear as he explained he had a contact in the police force who told him someone had pointed the finger at him. I looked at the lighter hoping it wouldn't be used as evidence in my own murder trial.

"Do you know who it is?" I asked, nervously wondering if I'd been lured to the pub on false pretences.

Looking over towards the exit, I knew there was no way I could make it without being manhandled to the ground. My only hope of escape would be to jump through the window pane and hope I didn't receive any life-threatening lacerations.

Over Humpo's shoulder, I noticed a familiar figure. It loomed up and towered over the pair of us.

"This is your informer," announced Weggy pointing at me.

The words sent a shockwave through my body. My addled brain struggled to compute whether it was a question or a statement as I prepared to execute my rudimentary escape plan.

Time seemed to slow down. For a moment, I was transfixed by Weggy's large tattoo of a heart, impaled by three daggers, on the underside of his forearm. The middle dagger was larger than the other two and had the name Carol inscribed on its blade. The smaller ones, on either side, had the names, Sian and Stacey.

"Yes," said Humpo.

Adrenaline surged through me as I discreetly edged halfway off my chair hoping there was enough strength in my legs to propel me through the glass. I visualised myself landing on the pavement outside before sprinting off down the road as Humpo and Weggy peered through the shattered window.

However, my mind wouldn't allow me to picture such a heroic getaway for long. Instead, it preferred to show me thudding into the window, sliding down the unbroken glass and landing in a crumpled heap on the floor whilst Humpo and Weggy silently watched on.

"If it hadn't been for him exposing that fokkin bastard Hugo for what he really was, our family home would have been sold by now."

Weggy offered his hand.

"Me and my brother owe you big time."

Bemused, I reached out and shook it.

"Let me get some drinks in first — I want to hear all about it — same again?"

By the time he came back from the bar and pulled up a chair my heartbeat had almost returned to normal. After taking a big swig of my drink, I began to explain the episode in The Momtaz, where my suspicions were first aroused.

"So, you saw him with another woman and you didn't think to tell AJ," said Humpo, making no attempt to disguise his annoyance.

"It wasn't as simple as that."

Reluctantly, I explained the incident with the chillies, which resulted in the pair of them exploding into laughter whilst clinking their drinks together.

"You are something else," smiled Weggy.

After the laughter died down, I went on to explain how I'd seen Hugo and his lady friend planting the mysterious vegetation around the cottage. The smile on Humpo's face disappeared.

"Hang on a minute — are you telling me you spent the night with my princess?"

"Well, yeah, but nothing happened. I mean, I didn't try anything. It wasn't like that. She asked me to stay."

Humpo struggled to control his rage. Sensing imminent danger, I quickly explained the circumstances which led me to be in AJ's bedroom. Weggy, aware of the potentially volatile situation which was developing, chipped in.

"Well, it's a good job he did spend the night with AJ, otherwise Hugo may well have got away with it."

Humpo looked at the pair of us for what seemed like an eternity. Finally, a smirk appeared on his face.

"I suppose you're right," he said raising his glass, "cheers, Fudgey lad."

We all clinked our glasses together.

"But if you ever mess her about…"

"I won't. I promise."

Weggy chuckled.

"I'm sorry, but I can't get the image out of my head of you in your chef's whites splashing water on your cock."

"If you think that's funny, you want to hear about the position I caught him in earlier"

"Let me get some more drinks in first," said Weggy.

A short while later, I watched him skilfully negotiate his way back from the bar, holding a tray full of drinks. Six pints of cider and six shots of sambuca arrived at the table.

"Here you go," he said handing out the drinks.

Humpo raised a shot glass.

"To Fudgey — my knight in shining armour."

We touched our glasses above the centre of the table then slugged back the aniseed-flavoured liqueur.

"Well, I was more like a knight in a shining wheelchair."

"To the knight in a shining wheelchair," proclaimed Weggy holding up his second shot of sambuca.

"Right," he said slamming his empty glass down, "tell me, what could be more embarrassing than getting caught red-handed washing your burning cock under the cold tap in the gents toilet of The Momtaz?"

Knocking back my sambuca, I felt a warming sensation as it glided down my throat. A woolly numbness rose from my stomach which seemed to shield me from any embarrassment as Humpo began to describe what he'd witnessed on top of the stairs.

Weggy struggled to grasp Humpo's version of events and I found myself constantly interrupting as I tried to explain the backstory.

After the pair had enjoyed a good laugh at my expense, I tried to put a stop to proceedings.

"Anyway, enough of all this, how about I carry on reading your palm?"

Weggy continued laughing. Humpo didn't. And after an uncomfortable pause, he declined my offer, preferring to persuade his brother to have a reading instead.

Once again, an upturned palm was thrust across the table.

"Go on — surprise me."

Gutted I wasn't able to probe Humpo further, I begrudgingly took hold of Weggy's hand and tried to be enigmatic. Leaning in to take a closer look, I was alarmed to see two sets of lines before realising I had the early onset of double vision. Squinting at his hand, I struggled to think of something to say. I glanced at his tattoo.

"You've got a missus called Carol."

"Everyone knows I've got a missus called Carol," he scoffed.

Allowing myself a quick peek at the two smaller daggers, I set about performing an elaborate and intriguing study of his palm.

"You've got two children — girls — Sian and Stacey."

Weggy seemed impressed for a moment until Humpo piped up.

"You idiot! Look," he said, pointing at his tattoo, "he's not reading your palm, he's reading your fokkin arm. I knew it was bullshit."

As they delighted in mocking my abilities, I was consumed by rampant anger. Putting my hand in the air to silence them, I tried to speak with some authority.

"Ok, Weggy, you want me to tell you something that nobody else would know?"

"Oh, yes please," he teased.

Desperately trying to think of something dramatic to say, I bought myself a few extra seconds by reaching for the cigarettes. Clasping one with my lips, I pulled it free from the packet. Weggy, keen for me to begin, produced his lighter and lit the end, reminding me of the episode in the public toilets.

"There is another name."

The sniggering coming from the two men continued as I concentrated on a random area of his palm.

"Come on, what's this other name," goaded Weggy.

Doing little to hide my annoyance, I looked up.

"George."

I felt Weggy flinch slightly. Tightening my grip on his hand, I shuffled closer.

"No, it's not George. It's a foreign name."

Looking up, I saw a disbelieving Weggy squirming in his chair. Revelling in his discomfort, my eyes darted between his hand and his face until I couldn't prolong the silence any longer.

"Who's Georgio?"

Weggy snapped his hand back.

"What a load of bollocks," he said flustered.

"I'm only telling you what I can see in your palm."

"Ooh, who's Georgio?" Humpo taunted.

Weggy made it clear he didn't want me to continue the reading so I took the opportunity to excuse myself and made my way to the toilet.

Glad of the support of my crutches, I wobbled unsteadily across the pub. There was no need to act this time. The rough cider and sambucas took care of that.

On my way back, I looked across the pub and out through the window. The light outside had faded and only the last few murky grey wisps of twilight remained. My attention was drawn to Humpo and Weggy who were both holding their hands in the air examining their palms. They spotted me returning and quickly put them down. Pretending not to notice, I made my way back to my seat.

"Right, who wants me to carry on reading their palm?"

A smile spread across my face as I watched them both shrivel back into their seats.

"Erm, I'd love you too, but I've got to go. Nice to meet you," said Weggy getting to his feet and hesitantly offering his hand.

I shook it firmly.

"Oh, hang on," I said, pretending to be intrigued by the lines on his wrist.

"Maybe next time," said Weggy whipping his hand from my grasp and disappearing into the throng of revellers.

I turned to Humpo. Avoiding eye contact with me, he stood up and began placing all the empty glasses on the tray.

"I'll get another round in."

Left alone, I began to feel the room gently spin. The effects of the rough cider and sambuca had crept up on me at first, but now I knew I only had a short amount of time before the lighter became my only memory for the rest of the evening.

Humpo arrived back with the tray fully laden.

"It's four deep at the bar so I thought I'd get a few rounds in."

Six shots of sambuca were dwarfed by six pints of cider. I knew the chances of me drinking my share were very slim.

"Tell me again, how did you end up in my daughter's bedroom?"

Feeling vulnerable, I began to explain. Humpo listened without a shred of emotion as I became increasingly paranoid. Convinced a raging fury was growing behind his impassive exterior I kept stopping at intervals to persuade him that no sexual advances were ever made towards his daughter.

"So, if it hadn't been for your daughter's kind actions, and allowing me to sleep on the floor, that shit bag would be a millionaire by now."

Sitting back, I waited apprehensively for his reaction. Humpo silently held up a shot of sambuca. Following suit, we clinked our glasses together.

"AJ speaks very highly of you. Helping her out with her assignment — comforting her when she was upset — getting off your sickbed and escaping from hospital to expose that cock sucker."

"I only did what anyone else would do in that situation," I said trying to sound modest.

A familiar busty barmaid appeared holding a small dented metal bucket which she emptied the ashtray into. She looked over at me and did a double-take.

"You're a good man, Fudgey lad. A noble man. A man of honour, integrity and decency."

"What! This dirty pervert?" exclaimed the barmaid.

"Dirty pervert?" repeated Humpo, "what do you mean?"

"The last time I saw this bloke he asked if he could see my tits."

"No, I didn't," I protested, "I just asked what sort of nipples you had."

Humpo sat opened mouthed as I hurriedly tried to correct myself.

"*Nibbles*. I meant *nibbles*. I was hungry. I asked her what sort of *nibbles* she had — behind the bar."

Humpo reached inside his jacket as I continued my frenzied denial. Half expecting a weapon to be produced I was relieved to see his hand return holding a couple of crumpled-up tickets.

"Alright, calm down, I believe you," he said ushering the barmaid away.

"I want you to do me a favour. AJ's been down in the dumps since she found out about that tosspot. She had been looking forward to going to The Caterers Ball with him."

"Oh, right," I said relaxing back into my chair.

"She'd bought a dress, booked in to get her hair done. You know, all that sort of thing."

He slid two tickets for The Caterers Ball across the table.

"I found these when I emptied the bin in her bedroom. I want you to ask her to go with you."

"Err, ok," I said watching him reach into his jacket again. He pulled out a bulging wallet and took out five crisp twenty-pound notes.

"Also, it's her birthday tomorrow," he said handing me the money, "get her something nice."

Humpo held aloft another sambuca. I did the same.

The pleasant tasting shot slid easily down my throat. Knowing I would struggle to remember much more of the night I decided to probe him again.

The background noise had increased gradually during the evening and I had to speak with a raised voice in order to be heard.

"Humpo."

"What is it?"

"I've seen your palm. What happened in the woods?"

Humpo held his hand up and looked at it in disbelief.

"There's no denying it," I continued, "I can see it in your lines. How else could I possibly know?"

A live band that had set up in the corner suddenly burst into life. The deafening sound of a distorted electric guitar filled the room.

Straining to hear him speak, I heard AJ's name mentioned.

"What?"

"AJ."

"Yes," I yelled.

My eyes fixed on Humpo's mouth as I waited nervously for the rest of the sentence. Concentrating hard on his lips as they formed each word, I failed to notice his attention had been drawn to the window.

"AJ — she's behind you."

Over my shoulder, I was surprised to see AJ outside, silently gesticulating with her arms to see if it was ok to come in and join us. We both beckoned her in and she disappeared from view, appearing at the table moments later.

After giving her dad a hug, she leaned over and shouted in my ear.

"How are you getting on?"

I put my thumb up.

"What are you doing here?" I shouted over the heavy metal band that was now in full swing.

Gleaning snippets of AJ's reply, I managed to deduce she had handed in her Behavioural Studies assignment, gone out for a few drinks to celebrate and was on her way home when she saw us through the window.

AJ could see I was struggling to hear and leaned down to shout in my ear.

"Do you fancy going somewhere a bit quieter? Just me and you."

Aware the lighter wouldn't be able to record anything above the deafening racket I nodded vigorously. She went over and shouted in her dad's ear which resulted in him standing up and shaking my hand. His lips moved but I had no idea what he was saying. As soon as they stopped moving, I put my thumb in the air and was relieved to see him do the same.

Once I'd retrieved the lighter and cigarettes from the table, I picked up my crutches and began to struggle through the crowd towards the exit. AJ walked in front, trying to clear a path, but I was still buffeted on either side by the increasingly raucous clientele. Outside, I was relieved to fill my lungs with the crisp night air.

"Where do you fancy going?" asked AJ.

The combination of alcohol and fresh air made my head spin and I leaned hard on my crutches as I drunkenly swayed from side to side.

"You look spangled."

"I do feel a little tipsy. I think I had a dodgy pint of rough."

"I think you've had enough to drink for one night. Come on, let's get a taxi, you can sleep at mine if you want."

"As long as there's no funny business," I joked.

Chapter Nine

Later that night, I woke up in semi-darkness, enveloped in a warm cosy duvet. Still feeling the effects of the alcohol, I lay listening to AJ breathing softly next to me. Without thinking, I snuggled up against her warm, naked body.

"And what do you think you're doing, Mr Fudge?" she whispered.

"Oh, sorry, I thought you were a pillow."

"A pillow?" she laughed. "It's ok, you can snuggle into me if you like."

I put my arm around her letting my hand come to rest on her cleavage. Waiting for a moment, I half expected it to be moved, but with no readjustment forthcoming, I casually let it wander downwards until it cupped one of her breasts.

AJ let out a soft, pleasurable moan as I sensually caressed her bosom. Becoming increasingly aroused, I allowed my hand to venture past her navel until it reached her loins.

Moments later, I was under the duvet. Accompanied by groans of delight, I kissed my way downwards, but no sooner had my eager tongue arrived between her thighs she gripped the hair on the back of my head.

"Fudge, have you got a condom?"

Reluctantly, I kissed my way back up her body until I re-emerged.

"Have you got a condom?" she asked again.

"No, I haven't, have you?"

She gave a sombre shake of her head.

"Oh, goodie."

Cursing my misfortune, I cuddled back into her as the first wisps of morning light penetrated through the curtains.

"AJ, I want to give you something," I said leaning over the side of the bed and reaching into my trouser pocket.

"I know you do, you horny beast."

"No, not that."

"What then?"

"These," I said waving tickets for The Caterers Ball.

"How did you manage to get those? It's sold out."

Tapping the side of my nose with my finger, I laid back down.

"Ask me no questions and I'll tell you no lies."

Nestling back into each other, we drifted off to sleep.

*

The room was full of bright sunlight when AJ's dad burst in singing *Happy Birthday*. He stopped abruptly when he noticed my head on the pillow next to his princess.

"What the fok's going on here?" he barked, noticing all our clothes strewn over the floor.

"It's ok, dad — I asked Fudge if he would stay the night and he very kindly agreed."

"Yes, I bet he did."

"I'm not naked," I lied, hoping to pacify the situation.

"If you were anyone else, you'd have left via the window by now."

"Dad, don't be like that, it's my birthday."

Humpo thought for a moment.

"Ok princess, do you fancy a fry-up?"

"Yes, please," I joked.

"Not you."

"Oh, go on dad, make him one as well. Look what he's got me, tickets for The Caterers Ball," she said brandishing them with excitement.

"That's very kind of you, Fudgey lad," he said, giving me a knowing look, "now can you kindly get out of my daughter's bed before I drag you out."

Once her dad had left the room AJ lifted the duvet and peered down.

"Not naked hey?"

"Well, I have still got my socks on."

*

Twenty minutes later we were sat, fully clothed, at the kitchen table eating breakfast.

"So, what time does The Caterers Ball start tonight, darling?" Humpo asked.

"Eight o'clock, flower," I said playfully.

"I wasn't asking you."

"Come on dad — lighten up. He was only joking."

"Oh, very funny. Anyway, Fudgey lad, do you fancy coming round here before the ball tonight to have some birthday drinks with AJ?"

Knowing it was more of a request than a question, I politely agreed.

"I could come and pick you up about six o'clock if you like."

"That would be great, thanks."

Finishing my breakfast, I hoped Humpo would offer me a lift home on his motorbike. But after dropping a number of hints he seemed more interested in fussing over the birthday girl. I was still optimistic when I asked him if I could use the landline to ring for a taxi.

"Yeah, sure. It's in the hallway."

*

The honk of a horn outside signified the arrival of the taxi and I said my goodbyes to AJ, who was excitedly unwrapping her presents at the kitchen table.

"I'll see you out," said Humpo.

As I went to open the front door, he grabbed my arm.

"Don't forget to get some nice presents."

Reassuring him there was nothing to worry about I made my way outside and clambered into the back of the taxi. After a detour to drop the lighter off at the police station I arrived home to find Bull lying on his bed, squinting at The Racing Post.

"Alright, mate, you're still alive then — how did it go last night?"

After giving him a brief overview, I fully expected him to comment on my brief dalliance with AJ's nether regions, but he just casually looked over the top of his paper.

"Humpo's given you one hundred pounds?"

"Yes, to buy AJ some birthday presents."

"Have you still got it?" he asked excitedly. "There's a horse running today that's a dead cert."

"I am not gambling it on a horse. Her dad will kill me."

"Mate, he won't know, this thing cannot lose. It's even money — put one hundred pounds on and we'll get two hundred pounds back."

"Bull, you don't understand. He *will* kill me." I paused for a moment. "What do you mean, '*we'll* get two hundred pounds back'?"

"I mean *you'll* get two hundred pounds back. Well, maybe I can get a small cut of the winnings, but we can discuss that later," he said as he got to his feet unfazed by my reluctance.

"Come on, the race starts in ten minutes."

Again, I refused his proposal but found myself being swept along by his enthusiasm. I continued my protestations as we hurried along the road towards the betting shop.

"It's fate," Bull said over his shoulder as I tried to keep up with him. "I've been keeping my eye on this horse for months. The trainer keeps running it over five furlongs. It always finishes strongly, but never quite wins because the race is too short. Finally, he's running it over seven furlongs today."

Bull's confidence was infectious.

"I was lying there thinking it's just my luck we're all skint until our student grant cheques clear next week. I prayed for a miracle and you walked in with one hundred pounds. I'm telling you, Fudgey, we'll be drinking champagne tonight."

We arrived at the bookies just as the horses were being loaded into the stalls.

"Quick, give me the money," said Bull holding out his hand as he scribbled down the bet with the other.

Without a second thought, I handed over the five twenty-pound notes and watched Bull hurry to the counter.

The cashier took the money and rang through the slip. Bull turned around waving it in the air with a big beaming smile on his face as if the horse had already won. The race started and I sat down on one of the tall stools opposite a large TV screen.

"That was a bit of luck. We nearly missed it," said Bull sitting down on the stool next to me.

"What's it called?"

"Egyptian Milly — the jockeys wearing white silks. There it is at the back."

"Oh, goodie."

"Don't worry, it finishes like a rocket."

Up to this point, Bull's confidence had overpowered my rational thought, but the consequences of the horse losing slowly began to dawn on me as it fell further behind. Thoughts turned to Humpo and how he might take the news that I'd gambled away his daughter's birthday money.

"Fok me, the jockeys using the whip already," said Bull.

My eyes fixed on the horse languishing at the back as the commentator confirmed Bull's observations.

"And at the back of the field, the jockey has already got the persuader out on Egyptian Milly."

"Fokkin hell, Bull, Humpo's going to kill me."

"I don't know what's the matter with it. It must be lame."

Falling into a dream-like state, I watched helplessly as the race played out in front of me like a slow-motion car crash. The sound of the leaders' hooves drummed rhythmically through the speakers as if hammering the final nails into my coffin.

Somewhere in the distance, I heard the commentator say, "and Egyptian Milly is moving up through the field."

Bull jumped off his stool and moved nearer to the screen.

"Come on, Milly."

One horse had gone ten lengths clear of the chasing pack as they entered the final two furlongs. I was drawn back from my trance to see our horse moving through the field into a distant second place.

Entering the final furlong Bulls tip was five lengths behind. The white silks of the jockey moved vigorously in pursuit of victory.

The commentator added to the drama. His voice grew louder with every stride until he was practically screaming in disbelief as Egyptian Milly closed the gap on the leader.

Wrenched from the depths of despair my emotions rocketed skywards towards unbridled elation as they went past the half-furlong pole.

I thought I was going to pass out when both horses flashed past the finish line together. Bull turned to me.

"Did it get up? I can't see properly without my lenses."

"I don't know."

My heart felt like it was pounding in my mouth.

An announcement came over the speakers, "photograph, photograph."

"What does that mean?" I asked.

"It was that close they need to look at a photograph to see which horse crossed the line first."

Our agony was prolonged for a few more minutes. As we waited for the result to be announced the TV screen showed endless replays of the finish. After watching the first one, we were convinced our horse had just poked its nose in front on the line. The next replay convinced us it hadn't.

With my fingers tightly crossed, I paced up and down the shop. Bull kept staring at the screen. He knew the result would be displayed on the TV before it was announced over the speakers. A few moments later, the quiet, which had descended in the shop, was pierced when Bull shouted, "bollocks!!"

It was only one word, but it was enough to confirm my worst fears. I walked unsteadily towards the exit — a brief, painful look at the screen confirmed Egyptian Milly had indeed finished second. Outside, I threw up on the pavement.

Bull followed, standing a safe distance away until I'd finished bringing up my breakfast.

"Sorry mate, a few more strides and he'd have won."

The words gave me no comfort as I wiped my mouth with the back of my hand.

"How the fok am I going to buy AJ's presents now?"

We trudged back along the road we'd hurried down moments earlier. I was silent under a growing cloud of despair. Next to me, I could hear Bull berating our misfortune from the poor start to the unlucky finish, but my thoughts were elsewhere.

"How much money have you got, Bull?"

"Fok all, until the cheque clears. How about you?"

Putting my hands in my pockets, I pulled out a few coins.

"Three pounds, sixty pence."

"Well, that's a start. At least you've got enough for the wrapping paper and a birthday card."

I let out a nervous laugh then stopped abruptly.

"That's it, Bull — as long as he *thinks* I've bought her presents…"

*

Later that afternoon, I sat at the kitchen table. In front of me were a couple of rolls of pink wrapping paper, a birthday card, a pair of scissors and some sticky tape. On the floor was a large, empty cardboard box, which according to the thick black lettering on the side used to house '100 x double quilted toilet rolls'.

I held a bouquet of flowers and was desperately trying to peel off the 'reduced to 99p' sticker when Bull came in holding a shoebox.

"Here you go, mate," he said placing it on the table and lifting off the top.

Peering inside, I saw an old pair of trainers.

"What are these for?"

"You'll need something to put in the box to give it a bit of weight."

"Oh, right."

"Are you sure this is going to work?"

"I just need Humpo to *think* I've bought her something. There's no way I'll be able to carry this massive box on the back of his motorbike. I'll have to leave it here. Then I'll get AJ something when my grant cheque has cleared."

Putting the lid back on, I wrapped up the shoe box and placed it into the larger one.

"I could do with a few more things to put in."

Bull walked over to the sink and picked up the plug and chain that sat on the window sill.

"How about a nice necklace?" he asked, letting it dangle from his fingertips.

"Give it here. I'll have to buy her a real one. Are you going to The Caterers Ball tonight, Bull?"

"Yes, mate. I'm sorry, but all the tickets have sold out now. I would have got you one, but to be honest, I thought you'd still be in hospital."

I told him about the tickets I'd been given as I wrapped up the plug and chain.

"That's great news. Jim and Micky should be back soon so we can have some early drinky poos."

"Well, as long as it's before six o'clock. AJ's dad is coming to pick me up for some birthday drinks at their place. What else can I wrap up?"

Bull crouched down by the sink and rummaged through the cupboard underneath.

"You've got the shoes — you've got the jewellery — how about a nice top," he said getting to his feet. He held up a tatty old t-shirt that had been seeing out its remaining days as a cleaning rag. I nodded and he tossed it onto the table.

"That will have to do."

"Fudge," Bull said ominously, "I need you to do me a small favour."

"What is it?"

As I concentrated on finding the start of the sticky tape with my fingernail the plate with the turd and mashed potato slowly slid into my peripheral vision.

"Fok off."

"But, Fudge, I can't do it. Without my lenses I won't be able to," he paused, "well, see my lenses."

"For fok sake. Maybe later."

After getting changed into a cheap suit I sat back down at the kitchen table. In the middle was the large cardboard box. It looked impressive wrapped in pink paper. Resting on top was a bunch of flowers and a sealed envelope containing the birthday card I'd written. Holding a knife and fork, I looked up at Bull, Micky and Jim standing a safe distance away in their suits, swigging cans of lager. Bull offered some words of encouragement as I looked down at the plate in front of me.

"I need a few drinks before I can do this," I said putting down the knife and fork.

Bull handed me a can.

"Get that down you. Do you fancy a few shots? I've got a bottle of peach schnapps."

After rounding up a random selection of glasses we headed into the lounge.

"Whose birthday is it?" asked Jim as he walked past the table.

"AJ's."

"Oh no, not that bird from The Freshers Ball."

"Yeah," said Bull, "he only ended up at her place again last night — slurping her love juices."

Jim could hardly contain himself.

"What! You drank from the hairy cup?"

"Well, it was more of a sip, but she tasted delicious."

"Dear me, Fudge, are you loved up? It's one thing having a drunken fumble, but buying her birthday presents!"

Over the laughter, I explained about the one hundred pounds, the dead cert and what was actually wrapped up on the kitchen table. Bull tried his best to look sheepish.

"How much more of this peach schnapps do you think you'll need before you're ready to look for my lenses?"

"You better just give me the bottle."

Bull handed it to me and I slugged on it until I felt my stomach begin to resist.

Almost unnoticed, Jim left the room muttering something about going to use the toilet. He returned shortly afterwards with a smirk on his face just as I was draining the last few drops of schnapps from the bottle.

"Right," I said sternly, "I shall return with your lenses."

There was a chorus of cheers. Bull patted me on the back and wished me luck as I made my way back into the kitchen. Sitting back down at the table, I picked up the knife and fork and started to tease apart the faeces. The back door swung open.

"Fudgey lad."

The faint smile on Humpo's face soon vanished when he noticed the plate in front of me.

"I can explain everything."

Crippled by panic, I figured my best option was to start by telling him about the extra hot sauce Bull had on his kebab the previous night. But before I could try to talk my way out of the dilemma, I was faced with another.

"It's ok — I'm a bit early —you carry on and finish your dinner."

Smiling meekly, I felt a small amount of sick rise from my stomach and enter my mouth. Looking down, my mind whirred, desperately searching for a way out.

"Come on, eat up, we don't want to keep my little princess waiting," I was just about to say I'd lost my appetite when Humpo continued, "if you don't want it, I'll have it. I'm starving."

Reluctantly cutting off a bite-sized chunk of the *sausage*, I brought it to my lips and shut my eyes.

"What the fok are you doing?"

My eyes sprang open to see Bull aghast in the doorway.

"Fudge, what the fok are you doing?" he repeated. "Please tell me you weren't about to eat that."

Bull followed my gaze as I looked towards Humpo.

"Oh, hello AJ's dad."

He looked back towards me.

"I was just going to eat my dinner before I go out — Humpo said he would eat it if I didn't."

Bull looked into my pitiful eyes.

"Well, I've got bad news for both of you, that's *my* dinner," he said giving me a slight wink, "you said you didn't want bangers and mash."

"Sorry mate, I didn't think you wanted it."

"Well, I do," he said ushering me out of my chair and sitting down in my place.

"Go on, you better not keep the birthday girl waiting."

Humpo strolled towards the table oblivious to our predicament.

"That's a big present, Fudgey lad, I hope it's one hundred pounds worth."

"Yeah, sorry it's so big."

I waited expectantly for him to question how we would transport it.

"It's a good job I've borrowed Weggy's van. There's no way we could have taken it on my motorbike. Come on, let's go."

Bull looked as horrified as I felt as I picked up the *present*, card and flowers. Outside, Humpo led me to a small green van that looked like it had been salvaged from a scrapyard.

"Are you sure this is road legal?"

"Don't worry about that, Fudgey lad, just put everything in here," he said struggling to open the back doors which were bent out of shape.

There was a high-pitched metallic screech as he eventually wrenched them open. A chill ran through me. It was the same sound I'd heard in the woods.

"Hurry up," he said impatiently, "what are you waiting for?"

I jolted into action and placed the *present* in the back of the van as I nervously scanned the shadowy interior. A dull metal object poked out from under a crumpled grey tarpaulin at the back. As my eyes adjusted to the gloom, I took a sharp intake of breath as I caught sight of the mud-caked tip of a spade.

"Come on, come on," Humpo urged.

I stepped away and he forced the doors shut — accompanied by another chilling squeal.

With my senses heightened, I got into the passenger seat. Humpo spoke at intervals. Deep in thought, I kept my interaction to a minimum — nodding, sighing and shaking my head as I feigned interest in the conversation until we arrived at the cottage.

Humpo leapt out and yanked open the back doors. The sudden shrill snapped me out of my trance. And before I knew it, I was holding the *present* and being shepherded into the kitchen. AJ was sat at the table, gently blowing freshly applied varnish on her fingernails.

"Oh, Fudge, you shouldn't have," she said looking up with genuine excitement.

"Happy birthday, AJ," I said placing the *present* in the middle of the table.

"Aww, thank you."

"Here's a card and some flowers as well."

"Thank you. Did my dad put you up to this?"

My eyes flicked towards Humpo who gave the slightest shake of his head.

"No, no, no. He just happened to mention it was your birthday today, so I thought I'd get you something."

AJ got up and kissed me on the cheek.

"Well, that's very thoughtful."

"But you can't open the present until after the ball."

"Why?"

AJ and Humpo looked at me quizzically.

"I can't tell you that. It will ruin the surprise."

She looked at her dad and I was relieved to see him shrug his shoulders.

"Do you mind if I just pop to the toilet?" I asked, hoping for a bit of respite.

*

Up in the bathroom, I took deep breaths vowing to let DI Cashun know about the van and its contents as soon as possible. The police station was not far from where the ball was taking place and I was confident I could slip out at some point to inform him.

As I walked back across the landing, I pictured Humpo being wrestled to the ground by a swarm of armed police, but my fantasy was interrupted when I heard a loud commotion erupt in the kitchen. Stopping at the top of the stairs, I listened to Humpo's booming voice fill the air with a barrage of swear words.

My heart felt like it was trying to escape from my chest as I tentatively made my way downstairs. A further volley of expletives rang out — I could only assume the *present* had been opened.

"I can explain everything," I said as I entered the kitchen.

Humpo was nowhere to be seen. The *present* was still wrapped up where I'd left it and the only sound was coming from AJ, who was sat hunched over the table, sobbing uncontrollably into her folded arms.

Before I had a chance to ask her what was going on a double-barrelled shotgun emerged from the pantry, quickly followed by an enraged Humpo.

"You fortune-telling tosspot!! Well, you didn't see this coming, did you?" he growled as he skilfully clicked open the barrels of the gun with one hand and began slotting two cartridges into the open chambers with his other.

"What have I done?" I squeaked as Humpo continued to arm his weapon.

With no reply forthcoming and fearing for my life, I made a bolt for the front door. Behind me, I heard a pitiful AJ pleading with her dad to stop.

As I entered the hallway an almighty blast bounced off the walls around me. With my ears ringing, I burst out through the front door and sprinted up the garden path before hurdling the gate at the end. Whilst in mid-air another deafening blast came from behind. A shockwave pulsed through my body and I landed in a heap on the other side.

Through the slats in the gate, I saw Humpo ejecting the spent cartridges from their chambers and begin to reload. AJ appeared behind him begging him to stop. Adrenaline surged through me. Unsure if I'd been shot or not, I sprang to my feet and darted into the night.

A few minutes later the adrenaline began to wear off and I allowed myself a quick look behind. Relieved to see the road was clear I slowed down to a brisk walk.

Chapter Ten

Arriving home via the back door, I headed straight for the phone in the hallway, dialled the number on the card I was holding and sat down on the stairs.

"Hello, DI Cashun, it's Fudge," I said, still struggling to breathe, "Humpo just tried to kill me."

The door to the lounge opened as I continued talking.

"With a shotgun..."

Bull, Micky and Jim huddled quietly in the doorway exchanging frightened looks.

"I don't know why…yes…at his place. Please, you need to get round there straight away and arrest him."

I fell silent, listening intently to the detective.

"Yes, I will. Oh, and another thing…he's got a van…his brothers…it's parked outside the cottage. I saw some stuff in the back…a tarpaulin, a spade…ok, I'll wait here…thanks, bye."

I sat looking at the receiver. Bull took it from me and placed it back on the phone.

"What the fok is going on?"

"I need a drink," I said getting to my feet.

They stepped aside as I made my way into the lounge and collapsed on the settee.

"Do you want some of this?" Bull asked handing me half a bottle of sherry.

After a few glugs, I started to explain but stopped mid-sentence when a car door slammed shut outside. Micky crept over to the window and peeked outside.

"It's ok. It's only one of the neighbours."

I continued to tell them how AJ's dad tried to kill me with his shotgun.

"I knew wrapping that *present* was a bad idea," said Bull.

"No, it wasn't the *present*. It didn't get opened."

"Hey? Well, what happened then?"

"Fok knows. I went upstairs to use the toilet and all of a sudden, I hear Humpo going crazy in the kitchen. Naturally, I assumed AJ had opened it, but when I went back down, she was sprawled over the table crying her eyes out with the *present* still wrapped up. The next thing I know, her dad comes out of the pantry and starts firing his shotgun at me. I can't understand what happened, I only left the room for a few minutes. It just doesn't make sense."

We all came up with different theories until blue lights silently flashed through the window.

Micky opened the front door and DI Cashun strolled into the room holding AJ's birthday card.

"We've got him."

"Thank fok for that. What about the van?"

"Yeah, we've got that as well. Forensics will take a look."

"Did you find out why he wanted to kill me?"

"Yes," said the detective tossing the card into my lap.

Perplexed, I picked it up and read the inscription I'd written inside.

'To AJ, Happy Birthday, you're a diamond, lots of love, Fudge'.

But another line, which I had not written, had been added underneath. I read it silently to myself before reading it out loud.

"P.S. Shame about your smelly fanny."

"To be honest, Mr Fudge, I'd be tempted to kill you myself if you gave a card like that to my daughter."

"I did *not* write that!!" I protested.

"Well, someone did."

Jim cleared his throat.

"Sorry, Fudge, this is all my fault — I wrote it — I just did it for a laugh."

"Did it for a *laugh*? It nearly got me fokkin killed!!"

"Sorry."

"How? When? I sealed the card in the envelope after I wrote it."

"Earlier, when I said I needed the toilet, I sneaked into the kitchen and steamed it open with the kettle."

DI Cashun shook his head before turning his attention back to me.

"I need to get a statement from you, Mr Fudge."

We made our way into the kitchen. Relieved to see the plate was no longer on the table, I sat down and gave my account of events.

"I told you, sooner or later, he would make a mistake. I just didn't expect it to happen like this," said the detective as he shuffled the pages of my statement together.

"I need to take this as well," he said picking up AJ's birthday card, "evidence."

"What happens now?"

"Well, at the very least, we can do him for attempted murder. He will argue that he was provoked, but at least we've got the van now. Hopefully, we'll find some DNA, then we can throw the book at him."

"Have you had a chance to listen to the lighter yet?"

"Oh yes, about that," he said leaning back in his chair.

"The sound quality wasn't the best, but there were a couple of things that interested us."

I waited expectantly for him to continue as he put his pen away.

"Like the time you ended up washing your cock in the sink at The Momtaz — and the time Humpo caught you naked, blowing softly into your friend's bum hole."

"I wasn't naked, I had my boxer shorts on, and anyway it wasn't like that, I was —"

The detective raised his hand in the air to stop further embarrassment.

"Unfortunately, everything else was inaudible, so it's just as well you stumbled across the van. Now we've got something to get our teeth into."

He stood up and made his way towards the back door where he lingered for a moment before turning around.

"If I were you," he said waving the birthday card in the air, "I'd go and explain to AJ about this."

I watched the door close behind him and pictured AJ crying uncontrollably at her kitchen table.

Bull came bounding in, "I found my lenses."

"You went through your shit looking for them?"

"No," he said holding up a glass of water, "they were in here. I found it under my bed. I must have put them there when I was pissed. Probably worried I might have drunk them in the night."

"Thank fok for that."

A shamefaced Jim appeared behind him.

"All sorted?"

"No, it is not all sorted. You're coming with me."

"Where?"

"We're going back to AJ's and you're going to tell her exactly what you did. Then you're going to apologise profusely."

It took further, more forceful persuasion before we began the long, slow walk to AJ's. Jim stopped at intervals along the way to try and weasel out of it, but each time I insisted, with increasing vigour, that he'd caused the problem so he should sort it out. Eventually, the silhouette of the cottage loomed upon us.

"There are no lights on, she must have gone out," Jim said hopefully, "come on let's go back."

"No."

Using only the moonlight to guide us, we walked carefully down the path. Stopping at the front door, I rang the bell, making sure the button came back out.

"Come on, she's not in," Jim said impatiently.

Bending down, I shouted through the letterbox.

"AJ, it's me."

"Come on, Fudge, let's go."

After ringing the bell a few more times I begrudgingly followed Jim back up the garden path. As we opened the gate, a voice came out of the darkness.

"Why?"

We spun around to see AJ's shadowy figure standing in the doorway.

"Why, Fudge?"

Her pitiful voice was barely audible.

"I didn't write it."

She edged back as I approached.

"I'm sorry, AJ, but I wrote it," said Jim over my shoulder.

"My dad's been arrested because of you."

"I thought it was because he tried killing Fudge," said Jim earning himself a dig in the ribs with my elbow. "Oh, err, sorry, yeah, it was because of me."

"They've taken away my uncle's van. They've searched the cottage. I don't even know what they were looking for. Why did you do it, Jim?"

He fumbled his way through a pathetic excuse as I watched on, hoping the distress etched on AJ's face would soften.

"I'm so sorry, AJ, I thought it would be funny. Anyway, Fudge said you tasted delicious."

"Ok, Jim, I think that's enough."

All three of us took part in an awkward pause before AJ broke the silence.

"Well, I appreciate you coming round to apologise, but because of you my dad has been arrested and charged with attempted murder. They weren't even real bullets, they were blanks."

Jim turned to me. "That's a relief — at least he wasn't trying to kill you."

"Oh, Fudge, can you tell the police it's all been a big misunderstanding?"

"Yeah, Fudge, tell them it's all been a big misunderstanding."

"Yes, thank you, Jim, you can go now."

He didn't need any further encouragement and hurried back down the garden path. AJ beckoned me inside and switched the hallway light on revealing her grief-stricken appearance in all its colourful detail. I was reminded of a sad circus clown and felt awful knowing that, once again, I was largely responsible.

"Come on, you can use the house phone. I've got a card with their number on," she said handing it to me along with the phone receiver. "Please try and get him released."

Holding the receiver to my ear, I stared at the name on the card and slowly dialled the number.

"Nobody's answering."

AJ looked like she was about to start crying again when a familiar voice spoke into my ear.

"DI Cashun."

"Oh, hello, it's Fudge…yes, I'm with AJ now…yes, Jim came with me to apologise. I just wanted to let you know that AJ said her dad fired blanks at me and asked me to ring you to see if you could drop the attempted murder charge."

AJ waited impatiently, trying to gauge the detective's response from my facial expressions. I tried to look disappointed as DI Cashun told me the charges were not going to be dropped and, if anything, there would likely be more serious charges to come once they'd examined the items found in the back of the van.

"What have you found?"

I was given the standard spiel about not being able to divulge information but was assured Humpo would not be coming home for a very long time.

"Oh…ok…bye."

Not wanting to look AJ in the eye, I turned away and replaced the receiver on the phone.

"Well?"

With my mind racing, I turned back around.

"Are they going to release him?"

"Erm, not yet."

"Why not?"

"They've found some things in the back of the van they want to question him about."

"What have they found?"

"He wouldn't say, but I'm sure it's nothing to worry about."

AJ broke down in tears and I found myself embracing her as she sobbed into my shirt.

I waited for her to catch her breath.

"I suppose the ball is out of the question?"

"Until my dad has been released, I don't fancy doing anything," she said without looking up.

"Come on, AJ, your dad will be out before you know it," I lied, "and he wouldn't want Cinderella to miss the ball."

There was no answer, she just squeezed me tight. Moments later, she lifted her head, and to my surprise, began to laugh through her tears.

"I'll need to wash your shirt first."

Looking down, I saw AJ's face imprinted on it like a child's drawing of the Shroud of Turin.

"Sorry about that."

"Don't worry about it. So, what about the ball?" I pressed, eager to salvage something from the evening.

"I don't know if I'm up to it."

"How about we have a drink while you think about it?"

"Ok," she said solemnly.

Leading me into the darkness of the front room, she effortlessly switched on a couple of table lamps. A large, antique globe took pride of place in the centre. AJ lifted the top half to reveal an array of bottles containing varying amounts of different coloured spirits and liqueurs.

"Crackerflaps," I said, trying to contain my elation.

"Under the circumstances, I'm sure my dad wouldn't mind us helping ourselves."

The tip of my tongue involuntarily ran between my lips as I moved in for a closer inspection.

"I can't believe Jim nearly got me killed."

"My dad was only pretending. He knew they were only blanks"

Still not convinced, I played along as I surveyed the array of drinks in front of me.

"Did Hugo get the shotgun treatment as well?"

"I hope so," she laughed, "I haven't heard from him since my dad went to confront him. I'm so glad you exposed him for what he really was, but I've got to be honest, my trust in men is at rock bottom at the moment."

"Well, you can trust me."

"I hope so, Fudge. Are you ok sorting some drinks out while I sort my face out?"

"Are you sure your dad won't mind?"

"No, he'll be fine. There are glasses in the kitchen and if you need any mixers there's lemonade and orange juice in the fridge."

Picking up a bottle of vodka I went in search of some orange juice. The unopened *present* still sat in the centre of the kitchen table next to an old photo album. The fridge door was dotted with novelty magnets. Some with serious-looking correspondence pinned underneath. One shaped like a banana had a letter underneath addressed to *The Executor of Mrs Kathleen Jones's Estate*. Another, shaped like a barrel with *I Love Scrumpy* on, held a letter from the local council. It was headed *Re: Certificate of Authority for Burial*.

I'd already finished my first drink and was pouring another when AJ returned looking slightly less dishevelled.

"Oh, Fudge, I hope my dad will be alright."

"I'm sure he'll be back home before you know it," I said handing her a drink.

Taking a big swig, she immediately began to wince.

"Blimey, Fudge."

"Yeah, it is a bit strong. I thought you might need something with a bit of extra oomph."

"Do you want to take that off?" asked AJ gesturing towards my makeup-smeared shirt. "You can wear one of my dad's t-shirts while I wash it for you."

After putting my shirt in the washing machine, she turned around and walked slowly towards me. Reaching out a hand, she gently caressed my pendant.

"You told me I was going to marry Hugo."

"No, I didn't."

"Yes, you did."

"I said you'd be married within a year."

AJ fell silent.

"Any chance of that t-shirt?"

She looked at me and smiled.

"Come on, follow me. Let's see if my dad's got one you can put on while you're waiting."

Humpo's room was filled with the smell of wax. It emanated from his trench coat which hung on the back of the door. Catching sight of it, I was instantly taken back to the night in the woods.

"What does your dad do for a living?"

"He's a gardener."

"A gardener?"

"Yeah, he loves it. I even came home late the other night and found him digging at the back of the cottage."

"What for?"

"I can't remember, I think he said he was planting potatoes."

"Oh, right," I said as alarm bells rang in my head.

My eyes darted around the room. There was an old metal-framed double bed, complete with a patchwork quilt. A lone chair sat facing the window with a small table next to it. On top was an ashtray full of cigarette butts, half a box of shotgun cartridges and an empty glass tumbler.

AJ walked over to a large mahogany veneered wardrobe. Slightly unnerved by the live ammunition, I enquired why her dad would keep shotgun cartridges in his room. She looked over at them and flippantly informed me that he would quite often sit in the dark with his shotgun waiting for foxes.

"Anyway, let's see if we can sort you out with something."

She opened the double doors of the wardrobe to reveal a few coat hangers and the rugged camouflage jacket which I'd seen him wearing in The Halloween Café. I wondered if the piece of folded-up paper was still in the pocket.

"See if there's anything in those drawers over there," she said, pointing at a sturdy-looking chest of drawers.

The first draw contained underwear and I quickly proceeded to the next, which to my relief, contained a selection of roughly folded t-shirts. As I picked one up something wrapped inside fell to the floor.

"Have you found anything?"

"Yeah, this," I said holding up an old teddy bear with one eye missing.

"What's this doing in your dad's draw?"

"It's probably an old one of mine. Bless my dad, he must have kept it."

"It looks like the one that missing girl was holding in the picture."

"Does it?"

"Yes, it does."

AJ's mood changed.

"Are you trying to say my dad has got something to do with that missing girl?"

"No — well — yes."

"Fudge, my dad hasn't got anything to do with it."

Her look of dismay was painful to witness, but I couldn't help thinking I was holding a vital piece of evidence. Putting it carefully back in the draw, I vowed to secretly inform DI Cashun as soon as the opportunity arose.

"Ok, ok. This t-shirt will do," I said, "come on, let's go and have some more of that vodka."

Back in the kitchen, I topped up our drinks whilst AJ opened a small drawer at the top of the washing machine and poured in some fabric conditioner.

"Right, it won't be too much longer. Let's go and get the fire started so we can dry your shirt when it's finished."

Nestling into the chair next to the globe, I watched AJ kneel in front of a pile of old newspapers by the fireplace. Taking a sheet from the top she expertly screwed it into a ball before turning to face me.

"Oi, you, get off your arse and come and make some of these."

"Alright, bossy-boots."

Kneeling beside her, I began crumpling sheets of old newspaper into balls as she set about sweeping the ash from the fire grate.

"One more should do it," she said.

Peeling off a final sheet, I began to scrunch it but stopped almost immediately. Slowly unravelling the beginnings of the ball, I stared at an appeal for the missing girl. A picture of Emily stared back at me. She was clutching a one-eyed teddy.

"AJ — it's the same teddy bear."

She leaned in for a closer look.

"No, it's not," she scoffed, before realising what I was implying, "why are you so convinced my dad is involved in the disappearance of that young girl."

"I'm not, I just, I mean it looks very similar. But why would your dad have a teddy hidden in his draw?"

"I don't know."

"Maybe, he'd been sat at his bedroom window one night, on the lookout for foxes. Something rustled in the darkness by the strawberry patch. Bang, bang. He fires a couple of shots, goes down to check the fox is dead, but instead finds the body of Emily still clutching her teddy."

This proved too much for AJ.

"Oh, Fudge," she said grabbing my balls and squashing them into the fire grate.

"I'm sure there's an innocent explanation to all this," I said putting my arm around her shoulders.

"Yeah, there must be."

"Come on, let's get this fire going."

After placing some kindling wood and a hefty log in the fireplace she lit the paper balls.

"Well, this is cosy," AJ said, as we sank into the sofa with our drinks and watched the fire crackle into life.

"Yeah," I said, gazing into the flames.

AJ snuggled into me and began looking at the lines on her hand.

"So, you still stand by your prediction that I'll be married within a year."

"It's not a prediction, it will happen," I said emboldened by the vodka.

AJ shook her head.

"Are you drunk?"

Looking at the remnants of my drink, I had to admit I did feel a little tipsy.

"Do you want me to pour you another?"

I followed AJ into the kitchen where the washing machine whirred away on its final spin.

Sitting down at the table, I watched as she poured more vodka into our glasses.

"Your mate, Bull, accidentally let it slip the other day you bought a book called *The Beginner's Guide to Palm Reading*."

"Oh, did he now."

"Yes, he did. He also told me it came with that necklace and pendant you're wearing."

AJ looked at me with raised eyebrows.

"I'm sure you told me your fortune-telling grandma gave it to you just before she died."

"Did I?"

The alcohol had lowered my guard and I freely admitted I'd only bought the book as a way of chatting up the ladies.

"I see, so you weren't interested in telling my fortune, you just wanted to get me into bed."

I gave a timid smile.

"But you must have some ability because you're so accurate. Would you mind reading my palm and telling me what the future holds?"

This was a no-lose gamble which I readily agreed to. I could say anything and she couldn't dispute it.

The washing machine finished its cycle and AJ took out my shirt. After hanging it on a clothes horse in front of the fire she quickly sat back down at the table and held her hand out.

"Come on, oh mystical one."

Taking hold of it, I was heartened to see her beaming smile.

"Look, you need to take this seriously. Trust me, I'm a professional."

Once again, I made a show of examining the various lines. Tilting her palm one way, then the other, accompanied by my familiar groans of intrigue.

"Leave it out, Fudge," she protested, "don't give me all that flannel, just tell me what you can see."

"I suppose you want to know how many kids you're going to have."

She nodded excitedly as I honed in on the small horizontal lines at the base of her little finger.

"I think you better have another drink. You're going to be a busy girl."

AJ frantically quizzed me as I poured out the remaining vodka.

"You see these four lines here?"

"Yeah."

"Well, each one represents a child. So, you my love, are going to have four children."

"Flippin heck," she said getting to her feet and instantly putting her hand on the table to steady herself. "Oh, Fudge, I feel a bit tiddly."

"Yeah, so do I," I said picking up the empty bottle, "I'm not surprised, this vodka's eighty percent proof."

Fearing the chances of going to the ball were dwindling, I suggested we checked to see if my shirt was dry.

Stumbling into the lounge, I fell backwards onto the settee, pulling AJ with me. And after a moment of looking into each other's eyes, we were soon locked in a long lingering kiss. I let my hand wander onto AJ's breasts and it was soon met with a playful slap.

"Come on," she said, "we'd better get a move on if we're going to this ball."

Begrudgingly hauling myself to my feet I went to feel my shirt.

"It's still damp."

"Don't worry, it won't take long in front of that fire. I'll get a taxi booked while we wait. I feel a bit more up for it now I've had that vodka."

AJ disappeared into the hallway before returning a short while later looking disappointed.

"I've rung all taxi numbers and everyone is fully booked. We'll have to get the bus, but the next one doesn't go for another hour."

"Oh well, do you think your dad would mind if we had a bit more of his booze?"

"Do you like brandy?" she asked pulling a bottle from the globe and waving it in the air.

"Nice one. We might as well tuck into that while we wait."

Sitting back down at the kitchen table, I poured two large brandies.

AJ caught sight of her reflection in the window.

"If I'm going to this ball, I'd better go and sort my hair out and get my dress on."

I followed her upstairs and lay down on her bed while she plugged in a hairdryer.

"I'm glad I'm a bloke. It's so much hassle being a woman."

"Yeah, you don't know how lucky you are."

"You don't need to go to all that trouble, you're beautiful just as you are."

AJ turned and smiled then turned on her hairdryer rendering further conversation pointless. I closed my eyes and waited for the low-pitched hum to finish.

*

When I opened my eyes again, I was slightly disoriented by the semi-darkness. I could see AJ lying next to me, fast asleep under the duvet. Rolling over, I planted my feet on the floor and slowly made my way across the room. Using the special technique to open the door, I crept out of the room and tiptoed into her dad's bedroom.

Reluctant to turn a light on, for fear of waking AJ, I put my hands on the bed and guided myself towards the wardrobe. Reaching inside his jacket pocket I felt the folded piece of paper. Quickly slipping it into my trousers, I shut the doors and stealthily made my way downstairs to use the phone.

"This is DI Cashun…"

"It's Fudge, I've found…"

"…I'm not at my desk at the moment, please leave a message after the tone…"

Disappointed, I left a whispered message, convinced my latest discoveries would help cement a conviction.

"What are you doing?"

AJ stood at the top of the stairs wearing her pink furry dressing gown.

"Err."

"Who were you on the phone to?"

Before I could think of a plausible excuse, she continued.

"It was the police, wasn't it?"

"AJ, there's something I need to tell you."

"What?"

"Come down here and I'll pour us a drink."

Sitting back down at the kitchen table we each clutched a freshly poured brandy.

"What is it, Fudge?"

"It's about your dad."

"What about him?"

"You know that girl that went missing?"

"Yeah."

"Well, your dad is the prime suspect"

She instantly began protesting his innocence.

"AJ, they think he killed her."

"Why? What makes them think that?"

I gulped some brandy.

"On the night she went missing, your dad was seen with a body slung over his shoulder."

"What? A body? Who saw him?"

Another gulp of brandy.

"Me"

"You!"

I nodded.

"You saw my dad?"

"Well, I didn't see his face exactly, but I saw his boots."

"*You saw his boots*!!"

I quickly explained the circumstances.

"They could have been anyone's boots."

"I saw his trench coat as well," I said trying to bolster my story.

"It could have been anyone's trench coat."

"I saw one of his hands — it was covered in blood."

AJ was relentless in her defence of her dad.

"I heard him use his Zippo."

"You *heard* him use his Zippo? Fudge, this is ridiculous."

"But it's true. And I heard a metal screeching sound similar to the noise your Uncle Weggy's van doors make."

AJ was becoming increasingly enraged.

"And what about this body he had over his shoulder, are you sure it was a body?"

"Well, I'm pretty sure."

"Pretty sure!! Did you see it?"

"Not exactly, it was wrapped in a tarpaulin."

"Well, how do you know it was a body?"

"Oh, come on AJ. A girl goes missing then shortly afterwards your dad is seen in the early hours of the morning with a large object wrapped in a tarpaulin over his shoulder."

"You must be mistaken."

"He was carrying a spade for goodness sake."

AJ's bottom lip began to quiver.

"But it's worse than that."

"How could it possibly be worse than that?"

"He's a hitman."

"What!! Don't be so ridiculous."

"And your Uncle Weggy is involved as well."

"What on earth makes you say that?"

"I saw the pair of them in The Halloween Café. Weggy handed your dad a picture of a man and told him to find him, do the business and there would be a big payday for him."

"I don't believe you. Is this some sort of sick joke?"

"I wish it was AJ. I watched your dad fold it up and put it in his camouflage jacket."

The phone in the hallway burst into life startling both of us.

She hurried to answer it and I soon gleaned DI Cashun was on the other end. It was heart-breaking to listen to AJ pleading her dad's innocence.

Retrieving the square of paper from my pocket, I opened it up and was bemused to see an article about the missing girl. Flattening it out on the table I felt a deep sadness as my gaze fixed on a picture of Emily.

AJ appeared in the doorway silently shaking her head.

"What?"

"They've found the missing girl."

"Oh no," I said, hunching over the table and putting my head in my hands, "where?"

"She was hiding in the attic at her boyfriend's mum and dad's house."

Struggling to compute what she had just said, I looked through my fingers at AJ, who had sat down opposite me.

"Apparently, she ran away after an argument with her mum."

"Hang on a minute, she's alive?"

"Yes, DI Cashun just told me."

"Are they sure it's her?"

AJ looked stunned.

"Yes, Fudge. They're sure."

Shaking my head, I struggled to make sense of the revelation.

"So, it turns out my dad didn't do it after all."

"But I saw him in the woods.

"On his way to bury someone?"

"Well, yeah."

She sat conspicuously silent.

"AJ? What is it?"

"Oh, Fudge, I really didn't want to have to do this, but what if I told you that's exactly what he was doing."

For the first time in her presence, I felt vulnerable. She made her way over to the fridge and removed the letter from beneath the *I Love Scrumpy* magnet.

"I don't understand."

"I promised my dad I would never tell anyone, but you give me no choice."

She took a big gulp of brandy; I did the same.

"Deep in the woods, there is a fallen tree that hardly anyone knows about. My gran used to go there whenever she wanted to relax. She would sit for hours on the trunk, just looking and listening. Immersing herself in the tranquillity."

AJ put the letter headed *Re: Certificate of Authority for Burial* on the table in front of me.

"What's this?"

"My gran said when she died she wanted to be buried under her favourite rose bush next to the fallen tree. When she passed away, I wrote to the council to get their permission to allow us to bury her there. That letter is their refusal. They said we could only bury her at a designated burial site."

"Oh no."

"We had no choice, Fudge. My dad was determined to carry out his mum's dying wish. That's what he was doing when you saw him."

"Fok me. So, your dad was carrying your dead gran over his shoulder?"

"No, you plum! My gran was cremated."

"Well, what was he carrying?"

"That was her favourite rose bush from the garden."

"But his hands, they were covered in blood."

"Have you ever tried digging up a rose bush?"

I didn't answer. In my head, I began to rearrange the same pieces of the jigsaw to form a totally different picture.

"My gran's ashes were in an urn. He had to do it in the early hours so no one would see."

"So, that's why your dad denied he was in the woods that night?"

"Yes, my dad made me promise never to tell anyone. It was to be our private place to go whenever we needed some solace. My dad didn't want to tell the police because he knew they would dig it up to double-check his story, then everybody would know about our secret place."

"Oh, AJ, I'm so sorry."

"It's ok, just promise me you'll never tell anyone else."

"I promise," I said clinking my glass against hers.

"So, what's all this about my dad being a hitman?"

Unsure what to say, I looked down at the newspaper article on the table.

"Was that from my dad's camouflage jacket?"

"Yes," I said picking it up, "but the piece of paper I saw had a man's face on it."

"What was it you heard my uncle say?"

"He said 'find him, do the business and they'll be a nice payout for you'."

I looked over the top of the article to see a beaming smile develop on AJ's face.

"You absolute plum!"

"What?"

"Turn it over," she said gesturing to the piece of paper I was holding.

On the other side was a picture of a man's blurred face. Only his eyes and eyebrows were in focus.

"That's the man he was after, Mr Blue," laughed AJ. "He's been on about that competition for ages. And you're right, if he found him and did the business, he would have had 'a nice payout'. All he had to do was say 'I know it's you, you're Mr Blue' and he'd have won a thousand pounds."

All I could do was shake my head as the monumental misunderstanding slowly sank in.

The feeling of relief started as a trickle but soon became a tidal wave. My torment was over and I couldn't have been happier.

"What's going to happen with your dad now?"

"DI Cashun said they can't release him until ballistics have confirmed the shotgun cartridges he fired were blanks. But that won't happen until tomorrow."

I looked at the clock. It was nearly midnight.

"So much for me taking Cinderella to the ball."

"It's ok. From now on though, no more secrets, no more surprises."

I nodded.

"Can I open my present now?"

"Erm, AJ."

"Yes," she replied, stretching out the word.

"There's something I need to tell you."

After embarking on a long-winded explanation, I concluded with an assurance I would buy some proper presents once my grant cheque had cleared.

"Oh, Fudge, what am I going to do with you?"

"Well, how about you take me upstairs and radish me."

"Radish you?" AJ laughed, "I'm not into any kinky stuff."

"Ravish, I meant ravish."

We staggered upstairs and collapsed onto her bed. Landing side by side, we stared into each other's eyes. A couple of seconds of silence was followed by a frantic period of kissing and undressing.

*

The following morning, I woke up, on my own, in AJ's bed. The smell of cooking bacon wafted into the room. Contented, I recalled the previous night's exploits which ended with a firework display of emotions exploding in my head as I exploded inside AJ.

Moments later, she came into the room wearing her pink dressing gown and holding a tray with two full English breakfasts on it.

"Morning, I've made you something to get your strength back, you horny beast."

"Wow, thanks."

"You're welcome," she said, adding, "last night was amazing."

"Yeah, it was. I know it's a bit late now, but did we use any protection?"

"Fudge, we didn't. We got carried away so quickly. One minute we were lying there and the next — do you think everything will be ok?"

Holding my hand in the air, I looked at the area just below my little finger and stared in disbelief.

"You know I read your palm yesterday and said you were going to have four kids."

"Yeah."

"Well, take a look at mine."

AJ stared at the four vertical lines at the base of my little finger.

"Oh my goodness — they're exactly the same as mine."

Printed in Great Britain
by Amazon

78045871R00123